MEETING THE DEVIL

ALSO BY H. BYRON EARHART

The Twin Destiny Series

No Pizza in Heaven

Faith Finds Forgiveness

Meeting the Devil

The Devil Deja Vu

Canterbury Canticle

MEETING THE DEVIL

BOOK 3 OF THE TWIN DESTINY SERIES

H. BYRON EARHART

Chula Vista • Columbus

Printed in the United States of America

Published by iCrew Digital Publishing

Website: icrewdigitalpublishing.com

e-mail: icrewdigital@gmail.com

Chula Vista • Columbus

iCrew Digital Publishing is an independent publisher of digital works. We support the efforts of authors who wish to independently publish in the digital world.

Cover Photos by Rick Lakin

❈ Created with Vellum

Printed in the United States of America

Published by iCrew Digital Publishing

Website: icrewdigitalpublishing.com

e-mail: icrewdigital@gmail.com

ISBN-13: 978-1-946739-01-8 (iCrew Digital Productions)

Chula Vista • Columbus

iCrew Digital Publishing is an independent publisher of digital works. We support the efforts of authors who wish to self-publish in the digital world.

❀ Created with Vellum

This book is dedicated to all the teachers who had the patience and persistence to nurture my appreciation for the diversity and richness of human life and culture.

PROLOGUE: STORMY WEATHER

Saturday morning Faith sat in one of their twin recliners in front of the picture window, sipping mint tea, gazing out over Lake Michigan.

She had gotten back to Chicago late Friday evening after a grueling ten days of country-hopping, one Hortonr Hotel after another—New York, Washington, Miami, and a handful of other cities. The corporate people handlers had mishandled the house-keeping people, and they faced the threat of a nationwide strike. Because of her previous success in solving labor problems, the top Horton echelon decided the best approach was for Faith to fly to the major hot spots and talk directly to the union reps. Faith had averted a strike and was satisfied with her accomplishment. When she reached the condo she was dead tired.

Scott got home at eleven after finishing several stories for the weekend paper. Faith went right to bed as she and Scott talked. She had looked forward to making love to him, but fell asleep in mid-sentence. She woke up Saturday morning to the sound of his electric razor, and called him back to bed. He said he had to run in to the paper early and proof a couple of articles in a special Sunday edition.

~

So, there she was, in her favorite lounger on a quiet Saturday morning, getting reacquainted with the lake she had missed so much during her travels. She needed to recharge her batteries. The bright sun warmed and soothed her tired body. The reflected beams off the water gave a double solar boost to her spirits.

She was home. Comfy. Relaxed. She set her cup down and felt herself dissolve in the luxuriance of a sun bath.

When she opened her eyes, she sensed a chill in her body and darkness in the room. Bluish-grey clouds covered the sun, blocking its light and heat. The water on the lake was roiled, gusts of wind whipping it this way and that. Without getting up, she grabbed a handy afghan and threw it over her legs, pulling it up to her chin. The warmth that returned to her limbs was soon followed by slumber.

Faith awoke with a start to a loud clap of thunder. The storm clouds were dropping sheets of rain to the accompaniment of repeated rumblings. She knew she was safe in her ferro-concrete condo, but she sat up, attuned to the lake and the violent forces unleashed on it. Directly in front of her, a bright flash of lightning streaked from the ominous clouds to the waves. Then a heavy curtain of raindrops obscured her view of the lake.

Deprived of her favorite scenery, Faith went back to bed, wondering if this stormy drama over the lake was sending her a message.

PART I
WHEN IT RAINS IT POURS

CHAPTER 1

Faith slept 'til midmorning and then showered and put her nightgown back on, topped with a terry cloth robe. Scott had said he'd be home shortly after noon, deadline for the Sunday edition.

It was after one when Scott opened the door. "You're still in your robe. Sleep all morning? You were very tired last night."

"I fell back asleep after you left. Sorry about last night. I looked forward to seeing you, and then when I hit the bed, ten days of non-stop negotiations just shut down all of my systems."

She walked over to him, opened her robe, and put her arms around him. "But I could make up for it now."

He had slipped off his coat and put his arms inside her robe. They kissed and moved to the bedroom.

"Turn the phone off, Scott. I don't want to be interrupted by any of Cal's last-minute editorial queries."

When they got out of bed, they noticed the flashing light on the message machine.

She laughed. "I knew your newspaper wouldn't let us have any private time."

He punched the play button. They heard not a Trib colleague, but Jeremy.

"Hi, Mom, Scott. This is Jeremy. We're in the car, on our way to Jon's. Kind of spur of the moment. If you're free, how about lunch Sunday at Oak Park? Just call Jon to let him know. I'm not sure if you got back from your trip. We'll settle for one or both of you."

Faith called Jon and accepted the invitation. Then Faith and Scott tended to some errands and shopping.

She wanted to eat at Happi Sushi that evening. It reminded her of the first time she took him to see her family, because they ate there the night before.

It was still chilly and rainy, so they had hot sake with their sushi.

They were still glowing with the sake when they taxied home, and Faith led Scott right into the bedroom. The contest to see who could undress first was a tie. They shared the prize in bed.

This evening Scott was the tired one, and Faith, well rested by her extra morning nap, got out of bed, slipping on her gown and robe. She leaned back in the recliner, peering out into the black of the night and the lake. No ship lights appeared. The storm continued. Suddenly a lightning bolt from sky to water illuminated dark clouds and rough waters.

Faith retreated to the warmth and security of bed and Scott.

CHAPTER 2

Faith and Scott saw Stephie looking out the front window when they arrived in Oak Park a little after eleven Sunday morning.

Stephie had the door open waiting for them, Mark and Beth close behind, and Stephie's little brother Jeb crawling at double time.

"We got big news for our newspaper, Grandpa Scott."

Scott humored her. "Hmm, what's the big news, Miss Chief Reporter?"

"Jeb's got a tooth!"

"Is that so? We'll have to have a story about that."

The kids were running through the house, chanting, "We're gonna do a newspaper, we're gonna do a newspaper."

Rachel was embarrassed. "Scott, we don't expect you to do a newspaper every time you come."

"No problem. I've finished my work. This is fun."

When the kids made another round, Scott intercepted them. "I know what we'll call this story."

"What?"

"The tooth, the whole tooth, and nothin' but the tooth."

Stephie giggled and led another charge of the youth brigade through the house.

She edited his title to: "Th' tooth, th' hole in the tooth, an' nothin' butt's tooth."

The adults joined in the laughter.

As usual, Faith hung back and let the children have their initial go at Scott, delighted he had captured their hearts. She got hugs from Rachel and Melanie and looked around. "Where are the guys?"

Melanie turned away. "They went for a walk."

"A walk? Where?"

"I don't know. Just out for a walk."

The kids interrupted them and Faith asked about helping get the meal ready and on the table.

When the guys got back Jon gave Scott a hand on the newspaper.

Faith joined Jeremy in the TV room. "I was surprised to get your call yesterday. Surprised, but glad. I just got back late Friday night."

"We hoped you'd be able to make it."

"You just decided to take off and come up?"

"Well, yeah, I guess so." He had walked to the window.

Faith looked closely at him. "Everything okay?"

"Yeah. Fine."

"How are you feeling?" She stared at him.

"I feel fine." He didn't meet her eyes.

"When was the last time you went to the doctor?"

"Just this week," he mumbled.

"Jeremy, I didn't have the chance to mother you when you were growing up, and maybe you're not ready for it now. But I can see you're not well. Your color's not good. I could see it even without comparing the two of you. If Jon walked in, I'd say you were a shade or two paler than him."

He nodded. "Well, you're right."

"If you don't want to tell me about it, just say so, and I'll butt out."

He sighed. "No, it's not that."

"Not what?"

"It's not that I don't want to tell you. It's just hard. And complicated."

Faith sat down, the worry lines creasing her face. "Tell me whatever you want to...it's serious?"

"We don't know. Not yet."

"Still running tests and...?"

"Yeah."

"And...?" She perched on the edge of her chair.

"Well, Mom, I'll let you have it, as direct and easy as I can. It's my kidneys. Especially the left one. They're not functioning like they should. My energy was down, I couldn't jog, so I went to the doctor and he said it was a good thing I came in."

"How bad is it?"

"It's hard to pin the doctor down, because he doesn't know. The left kidney is only operating at about twenty-five percent, the right one is working significantly better than that."

"And they don't know why?"

"No, like you guessed, they've been running some tests and have me on some medication."

"Hmm. And the trip? You're not getting a second opinion in Chicago?"

"No, nothing like that. I came here specially to talk it over with Jon. Because since we're identical, he may have the same problem. Or if he doesn't have it now, he may have what they call a genetic predisposition for it, a tendency or possibility or likelihood."

"Have they narrowed it down to several diagnoses?"

"Well, of course, the worst case would be cancer, although they have no evidence of it."

Faith's mouth was open but no words escaped.

Jeremy said, "Then it could be a tumor. Benign. In either case, they'd do a biopsy, and surgery would be likely."

"Or?"

"Well, kidney function and failure is still not fully understood. Sometimes it runs in families, hereditary. That's one reason, when the doctor heard I was an identical twin, he wanted me to notify Jon at once, and have him undergo the same tests as me. It's preventative for him, to help him catch it as early as he can. Of course, it's only a precaution, it may not have anything to do with him. Naturally, it's helpful for Jon to know about my diagnosis, in case he has something like this. And my doctor would like to have Jon checked, to see if my genetic double gives him a clue to my condition. If he has the same test results as me, then we have a common hereditary problem, and they can rule out hormone imbalance or infection.

"And if they can't identify a hereditary link, then it could be environmental, something I was exposed to, but not Jon. For the life of me, I can't think of any environmental problem, because I never worked with chemicals, heavy metals, radioactive materials, and things like that. The nurses and doctors ran me through a ton of questions about this: 'Did you ever work in a cleaning establishment? Were you ever exposed to carbon tetrachloride?' They quizzed me on a number of chemicals."

With eyes wide open, Faith said slowly, "Jeremy, you said one reason you came to Chicago was to talk to Jon."

"Yes."

"And another reason was to talk to me."

"Yeah. I didn't know how to break the news over the phone. It seemed better to drive up and talk to each of you. I was going to tell you, but you beat me to it, asking how I was, and I didn't want to lie about it."

Faith closed her eyes for a few seconds, then leveled her gaze at him. "I suppose you want family histories?"

"The doctors want to know as much as possible about the medical records of my family. I told them I'd talk to you."

The kids burst in. Beth was carrying Jeb in a bear hug.

Rachel announced, "Lunch is ready!"

"Jeremy, let's talk about this after we eat."

CHAPTER 3

Faith didn't have a chance to tip off Scott, but she read the faces of Melanie and Rachel, both quieter and more serious than usual.

Everyone got through the meal, made easier by the presence and chatter of the children.

When the newspaper had been delivered to everyone, Rachel and Melanie were busy clearing things away. This was the first chance Faith had to talk to Scott. "Jeremy has a serious health problem, and Jon may have, too. I'm going to have to tell them about their father. Scott, I need your support."

"Are you sure? Telling them about Doug?"

"No choice. Jeremy's doctors want family histories."

He bit his lip. "Well, I guess there's no other way."

The kids were parked in front of the TV for an hour of cartoons. Faith knew her time was limited. She walked into the kitchen where the twins and their wives were talking.

"Folks, I'd like you to sit down around the table while the children are busy."

The foursome exchanged wary glances as they filed into the dining room and took their seats.

Faith had worry wrinkles on her face, elbows on the table, chin propped in her right hand. Scott sat next to Faith, taking hold of her left hand.

The few seconds of silence were broken by the deep breath that exploded from Faith's open mouth. "I've got something to tell you. Jeremy talked to me about what all of you've heard, so I don't need to mention his condition. But to go right to the bottom line, he needs to know about family medical history, and so I have to let you in on something I thought I'd never live to tell you.

"My hope was that you'd find out about this after I was gone and buried. However, Jeremy's health changes all that. So, I've got to bring up something I didn't want to, and don't quite know how to say it. The only thing I can do is just give it to you as simply as possible."

She looked directly at Jeremy and then Jon. "When I first met you, I told you I didn't know anything about your father. I was young, inexperienced, and foolish. I only met him once, when I got pregnant. Well, that's not the whole story."

Jeremy frowned. "It's not?"

"No, Jeremy, what I told you then was true. But since then, the situation changed. After you guys found me, the image of your father appeared to me in dreams. Nightmares. And it bothered me. So much so that I had to locate him.

"Remember when I took a month off? That's when I started looking for him. Scott helped me. That's how Scott and I met and came to know each other. Father Whitmore helped, too. I can't go into details now, but eventually I saw him."

Jon gasped. "You met...our father?"

"Not exactly. Scott met him and talked to him, but without telling him about me. Or you two. So, to make it perfectly clear, your father never knew that...that one time...we were together...I got pregnant and had you. Scott helped me locate him so that we know about him, but he doesn't know about us."

Jeremy interrupted her. "I don't understand. You went to all that trouble to locate our father. And Scott met him. You saw him." He sucked in a deep breath. "And you didn't tell us."

"Yes, that's the hard, sad part of the story. We had a detective do the initial leg work, and your father's been married and divorced twice, and, in the detective's words, he's a womanizer."

Jeremy and Jon started to talk at the same time as Faith went ahead with her story.

"Let me try to finish this, then you can ask questions. It's painful for me, and can't be very pleasant for you.

"I'll put this as politely as I can. Your father doesn't seem to be a very reliable character. I didn't actually meet him last year, but saw him behave in a very...let's say...immature way and I reached the conclusion it would be better not to contact him and let him know he had twin sons. And it seemed best not to tell you about him. I discussed this with Scott, and he agreed. But I'll take the responsibility for that.

"So that's the gist of the story. The bottom line is that I drew up papers with my attorney giving you the information: who your father is, where he can be located, in case you ever needed medical records. I thought I'd never live to see this day. But it's here. And tomorrow, if you agree, I'll contact my lawyer and start the ball rolling to request medical records from him and his parents and siblings."

Faith's shoulders sagged. She had been holding Scott's hand, but now she put both hands over her eyes and began crying. She was shaking, and Scott stood up to move behind her and put both arms around her.

Jeremy was still nonplused. "Mother, I just want to ask— "

Melanie gave Jeremy a killer look as she put her hand over his mouth and stood up. Then she joined Rachel, as they walked to each side of Scott and hugged Faith. Scott stepped away so the two of them could enfold her in a clamshell embrace. They were crying softly with Faith. Jeremy and Jon, seeing their wives in tears, got up and edged their way around the table, each with an arm around his wife, the other arm touching Faith. The sight, sound, and feel of their sobbing mates got them crying, too, and as Scott rejoined the semicircle with his arms over the twins' shoulders, he shed tears with them.

This tear fest was in full motion, when the kids entered the room. The two girls, seeing their mothers crying, ran to them and buried their heads and sobs in maternal flesh. Mark put his arms around his dad and soon started crying, too.

The latecomer to this sob session was little Jeb, slowed down by his creep-and-crawl mode of locomotion. At the back of the pack, unable to weasel his way into the group, he let out a howl of a different order. The others were crying in unison, a chain of lament. His was a yell of complaint, an outsider wanting in on the joint effort.

His outburst was rewarded. Everyone stopped crying, turning around to look down at Jeb. Then they realized, from Jeb's lowly point of view, how odd they must appear, six adults and three children holding a spontaneous cry-in. When they looked at each other, the weep-in immediately changed to a laugh-in. Jeb, in mid-yowl, stopped, and as Rachel scooped him up, joined in the laughter.

The children didn't even ask what this was all about. They were used to the instant reversal from bawling to merriment. Their only question was voiced by Stephanie. "Mom, c'n we have some popcorn with cartoons?"

This got the adults to laughing again, and the younger set joined in, not knowing what was funny but enjoying the jollity.

Rachel put some popcorn in the microwave and reinstalled the offspring in the cartoon-viewing mode. Then the family council reconvened, with Rachel and Melanie urging Faith to go ahead and do whatever she had to with her lawyer, to get the medical records of the twins' father. Jeremy and Jon were eager to ask questions, but the dirty looks they got from their spouses stopped them short.

CHAPTER 4

On the drive home, Scott talked as Faith listened, drained from the emotional roller coaster.

"God, you've got a great family. I've never seen such a collective show of support."

She whispered, "Uh-huh."

"And little Jeb, that was fantastic. Do you remember the line from that song of the Bee Gees?"

I started crying,

And set the world to laughing.

"When Jeb gets old enough, I'm going to get him that song."

"Uh-huh."

She was so exhausted she napped the rest of the way into Chicago.

The next morning Faith sent emails to Horton people and her boss saying she'd need the day off for personal business, then left voice mail for her assistant, Linda, to have her handle a few details, reschedule appointments, and to call Faith on the cell phone for any emergencies.

She sent an early email to her attorney, too, giving him a heads up about her request for medical information. She supposed he wouldn't get to the office before nine, but if he did, he could pull her file and get out the documents.

She had set up her will and sealed papers concerning Doug with her long-time attorney, Bob Hawkins. When he moved to California, she got handed off to one of the younger lawyers, Ted Sorenson. She wasn't too happy with this arrangement, but she figured her affairs were in good order, and she didn't need any heavy-duty lawyering. Even a lightweight attorney would be adequate for her simple needs. Now she began to wonder.

She waited until 9:15 to call, giving him a chance to down the first secretary-made-and-fetched cup of coffee.

"Mr. Sorenson is not in yet. I expect him at 9:30. Shall I transfer you to his voice mail?"

"No. Just ask him to call Faith Armstrong as soon as he can."

"Does he have your number?"

"I'm one of his clients. Yes, he has my number."

When Faith had not received a call back by 10:30 she was steamed.

"This is Faith Armstrong. Mr. Sorenson, please."

"I'm sorry, he's on the phone. Could I take a message or do you want his voice mail?"

"No. Your senior partners are still Ludwig, White, and Franklin?"

"Yes, that's right."

"Then I'd like to speak to Mr. Ludwig, Mr. White, or Mr. Franklin. Preferably Mr. Ludwig."

"I'll see if one of them is available."

"Thank you. I'll hold." She only held a few seconds.

"Hi, Faith. Bill Ludwig here. How are you?" His baritone voice was coated with honey.

"Fine, Bill, thanks for asking. But you know this isn't a social call."

"Sure. At your service. What can we do for you?"

"I have an urgent matter, part of my will that Bob Hawkins drew up for me. It's something Bob and I never shared with anyone else in your firm. And I've been trying to get through to Ted Sorenson this morning, but he seems to be busy. So without going into the whole story now, I guess how you could help me is to tell me who will handle my legal work."

"Well...can you tell me a little more about what kind of legal work you need."

"It's in my file."

"Okay...you've got quite a file, anything in particular?"

"Yes. I need legal papers served on someone to produce his medical records."

"I see. Uh, that will take some time."

"I don't have much time."

"Does Ted know about this?"

"I haven't been able to talk to him yet."

"Do you want to talk to him? First, I mean?"

"Bill, I don't want to play musical lawyers. That's not what I pay you guys an annual retainer for. Can Ted Sorenson handle this kind of legal paper?"

"Any competent lawyer should be able to."

"I can't settle for competent and should. I want expert and will."

"Let me suggest this. I'll go down to Ted's office right now and see if he can start the ball rolling, and if that doesn't work for you, we'll get someone else in the firm to handle it."

"Okay. This came up over the weekend, and I took off work today to handle it. So I need to get on this right away."

Faith hung up, and knew she wouldn't have to take her hand off the phone. She could almost hear, across the expanse of the Chicago Loop, Bill Ludwig stomping down the hall and yelling at Ted Sorenson to call with an apology.

She waited for the second ring before answering. "Hello, Faith? Ted Sorenson. Sorry I didn't get back to you right away. The secretary didn't tell me it was urgent, and I didn't get through my regular phone messages yet."

"Have you seen my email?"

He stuttered. "Mm...email?"

"Yes, I sent you an email."

"Uh, when?"

"Early this morning."

"No. I haven't even started on email yet. Do you want to tell me what's up, or do you want me to read your email first?"

"No, that's okay. Let me ask you for a favor."

"Sure."

"Could you ask your secretary to pull my file and give it to Bill Ludwig?"

"Uh, well, I'd be glad to look at it, but...is that what you want?"

"Yes. That's what I want."

BILL LUDWIG AGREED to meet with her at 1:30, have the papers reviewed, and be ready to advise her on how to proceed. Faith was in the Ludwig, White, and Franklin offices at 1:15. It was still less than twenty-four hours since the lovely tear-fest and laugh-in. The combination of elation and exhaustion from the family gathering had given way to frustration. She felt she had wasted half a day and accomplished nothing.

At 1:20 when Bill Ludwig opened the outer door and strode into the reception area, he had his back to Faith, but the secretary raised her eyebrows and looked sideways in Faith's direction. The seasoned attorney, in his lawyerly three-piece suit and conservative tie, read the secretary's body language and turned to greet Faith with a smile and outstretched hand.

"Faith, good to see you. Be with you in just a minute."

Faith was reassured by the mature appearance of Bill Ludwig, his thinning and graying hair combed straight back, crow's feet at the corners of his eyes marking his many in-court battles and his numerous out-of-court negotiations.

A few minutes later, she was ushered into Bill Ludwig's office.

"Ted Sorenson felt bad about the delay this morning. But let's see what we can do to, as I said this morning, get the ball rolling. Let me try to get the picture straight. You're right, Bob Hawkins never told me about the sealed document. So you have twin sons, and you want medical records from the father. Is that what it boils down to?"

"That's the gist of it. It's a pretty simple request. But Ted Sorenson didn't seem to be ready to take care of it."

"And I suppose the reason you're asking us to obtain the records is that the father's already refused you and/or the sons."

"No. Actually none of us has asked him."

Bill raised his eyebrows. "And there's a reason why you didn't ask?"

"A bunch of reasons. Mainly because I only was with him once, when I got pregnant. And he doesn't even know he's the father."

"Hmm. Thirty years ago. And you never contacted him since...that one time?"

"No."

"And you didn't contact him...before...today? No, you already said you only met him once. Hmm." He peered at the ceiling.

"You're hesitating. See any problems? Bob Hawkins said all the papers were drawn up. Like I said, and Hawkins put it this way, too, a simple matter."

Ludwig forced a smile. "And drawn up well. For one purpose: notifying the boys about their father and his whereabouts, so that they could identify and locate him. But 'simple', no. As they say, the devil is in the details."

"So...? What details?"

"That takes us to another stage, whether it's you or one or both of your sons."

"Which is?"

"Asking him for the records."

"And what's so difficult about that?"

"Well, maybe it won't be difficult. Maybe we'll just ask Mr...?"

"Parnelli."

"...Mr. Parnelli to give us the records, and he will."

"Why wouldn't he?"

"Well, let me put it this way. I have to think there's some reason why you're asking us to request the records. Otherwise you'd just call him up yourself."

"Yes. Privacy, for one thing. And, to be honest, the guy is not too reliable. He's been in and out of several marriages and a number of relationships, so we, our family, would just as soon keep our distance."

"I'm beginning to get the picture. You want Mr. Parnelli to give his medical records to an unknown party or parties."

"I guess so."

Bill picked up his Mont Blanc pen and put the top against his lips. "Well, my question. again, is why would he do that?"

"And why wouldn't he?"

He grinned. "My dear Faith, three decades of lawyering have given me all sorts of reasons why people will and won't do things. Let me put it to you. If you received a request to reveal your family medical records to someone or ones who did not reveal themselves, would you?"

"I don't know. I guess it depends."

"Well, as your attorney, I certainly would advise you not to."

"And if you were Doug's, Mr. Parnelli's, lawyer?"

"Dead set against it. Potentially he'd be admitting paternity, and that would leave him liable for child support, who knows what. He could be sued to the hilt."

"I thought about that. We could state, what do you call it, stipulate...?"

He nodded. "Yes, stipulate."

"...that neither I nor my offspring by him want anything but the medical records. Receiving them would waive any claim of past or future payment."

"That's not bad, Faith. Not bad at all. Makes it less risky, in fact it reduces risk on his part. That is, if he will concede the point of paternity."

"We can prove it."

He frowned. "How?"

"DNA. A comparison of his and mine with the boys' DNA will prove he is the father."

"And you have a sample of his DNA?"

"No. But it's a simple test."

"We're back to home plate: will he or will he not give us a sample? It's about as personal a piece of property as you can imagine, and I don't think you'd be willing to give up yours. Again, I'd counsel against it."

Faith gasped. "What can we do?"

"Do you have any witnesses who could sign an affidavit or even testify to his paternity?"

She stiffened in her chair and scowled. "For heaven's sake! It wasn't a public event! I was young and foolish and made a mistake. No! No one else saw us."

Bill held his hand up to ward off her anger. "Faith, I'm not the bad guy, I'm looking at you, but I see three other people I may have to talk to. One is Mr. Parnelli. The second is his lawyer. The third is a judge. We have to be able to negotiate with the first two and maybe litigate with the third. To our advantage. So I have to ask the same nasty questions they're sure to bring up."

"Okay, sorry." She hung her head.

"So here's a tough one. How do you know he's the father?"

"Because I never had sex before I was with him, and several weeks later I knew I was pregnant, and nine months later I delivered the twins."

Bill looked down at his pen. "Okay. Understand, I'm not attacking your virtue. But if we go to court, the other lawyer will do anything to discredit you. That's why we've got to be sure about this, so he doesn't come up with some old boyfriend who says you had a thing going."

"There is no old boyfriend, and there never was a thing going."

"Fine. We'll drop that. Now tell me how you found Parnelli."

She gave him a brief version of the trail she and Scott followed, the detective's investigation, and the visit to Parnelli Construction Co. in Peoria.

"Hmm. Yeah. Well, that's a great job of investigation, discovery, but one of the tough double questions a tough lawyer will ask you is: Why didn't you tell Mr. Parnelli he got you pregnant, and why didn't you contact him during the past thirty years?"

She started to talk, but again he held up his hand. "No, don't bother to answer, I know the reason why now: the medical records. But a lawyer and judge may be tough on you."

Tension wrinkled her forehead and extended in double lines between her eyes. "Bill, I feel like I'm on trial here, and I haven't done anything wrong. Bob Hawkins didn't tell me this would be so complicated."

"As a part of your will, a post mortem notification to your descendants, no problem. But securing DNA, admission of paternity, and release of medical records, that's a different ball game. More than a double header, a triple header."

"Well, I'm lost. And you, the lawyer, are supposed to help me find my way out of this mess. In simple terms, what can you do?"

"The first thing I can and must do, and that's been my miserable job today, is to let you know how complicated and tricky things can be. Next, we plan strategy. How we can approach Parnelli. The idea about stipulating no claims in exchange for the medical records, that's good."

"Can we start with that?"

"No. We don't want to start with that, because we want to end with that. Part of legal strategy is to get the other side to give as much as they will and your side to give as little as possible."

"So where do we start?"

"I have to explore something with you. In negotiating terms it's quid pro quo: this for that, in simple terms. You want Doug's medical records. What does he get in exchange?"

"Well, the stipulation that he will never be asked for money or anything else."

"Personally, I can tell you that's a good point. But his lawyer will probably respond that you have no claim on him, financial or otherwise, so the stipulation is empty. The lawyer will say to his client the stipulation is useless: he can't eat it, bank it, use it. He doesn't owe you anything now, so a stipulation that he doesn't owe you anything has no intrinsic value for him."

"What can we do?"

"Well, you're smart, Faith. On your own, you've come up with what you're ready to give him. The other half of it is what you will not give him."

"Such as?"

"Access to you and your sons."

"Well, could we stipulate that?"

"No. That would not be wise."

"Why? It's what we want."

"It's what I call the Pandora's box syndrome."

"Pandora's box?"

"Yes. A lot of fairy tales have this or a similar mystery element: Whatever you do, don't open the box. And you know what happens."

"Sure. The character does what he or she is told not to do. And that's why we shouldn't approach Doug Parnelli with a refusal for him to meet us."

He nodded. "Righto. In fact, if we did, he might just be curious or devious enough to make delivery of the medical records conditional on a meeting. With you. Or your sons. Or, hell, he might insist on meeting all of you."

"I'm beginning to see how this works."

"Uh-huh. I don't know if you ever played poker, but you never want to show your hand or give away anything, even in a facial expression."

"I never played poker."

"Well, help me out here. I need to know who I'm playing against. Would you share the detective's report on Parnelli with me?"

"Yes, I can go home and get it now."

"Fine. I can't get to this until tomorrow. I have clients the rest of the afternoon. The detective's file will help me size up this guy and plan how to deal with him."

Faith taxied home, had the cabby wait for her, and went back to the lawyer's office with the detective's report.

CHAPTER 5

$\mathcal{F}$aith was impatient for Scott to get home, calling him at the office. "How long before you can make it?"

"I'm finishing the last article. Try to be there by seven. How'd it go with the legal eagle?"

"Complicated. And frustrating. I'll tell you about it over dinner."

"Want to meet me some place?"

"I'm too tired to go out."

"So?"

"Before you leave the office, order a pizza in, and I'll let the doorman know."

Scott arrived a few minutes before the pizza. They had just started to talk about the lawyer.

"I spent half the day getting in to see an attorney. The one Bob Hawkins passed me off to was not quite or just barely competent, so I went straight to the top and got Bill Ludwig."

Scott let out a low whistle. "He is the top."

"Yeah, but he gave me a lengthy tap dance about how complex and time-consuming it'll be to serve papers on Doug."

"You didn't expect him to tell you it would be simple and brief, did you?"

"No. But I didn't think he'd tell me it'd be almost impossible to get the medical records from Doug."

"Why not?"

"I thought Bob Hawkins had the paper work set up so that we could just make a simple request and get the records."

"No, Faith, what was simple was leaving the sealed record for the twins, to let them know who and where their father is. Getting records is a different matter."

"That's the gist of what Bill Ludwig told me."

"What does he recommend?"

"He asked for the detective's report, to learn as much as he can about Doug, to figure out how best to approach him. I came back home and got the papers and dropped them off."

"Anything more specific?"

"He said we'd probably just ask for the records. Then he and his lawyer will probably say no, and then we can state, stipulate, that if he hands over the records, neither I nor my offspring will bother him for any money."

"Well, I have a suggestion for that stipulation. Namely, each party releases the other party from any claim to damages or remuneration."

"That's good, Scott. I see what you mean. It protects Jeremy from any frivolous lawsuit."

"Damn right. Anything else?"

"Well, he said we, the boys and I, should be clear about what we are willing to give and not give in the negotiations. I wanted to stipulate that neither I nor the boys would have to meet Doug."

"What did he say?"

"It'd be a mistake to even mention it, because then Doug might make it a condition of handing over the records. Bill said it was a kind of wanting what you're told you can't have."

"You wouldn't actually meet with Doug, would you?" His voice had an edge on it.

"Not if I could help it."

He said, "You can help it. Just refuse to meet him."

"Well, Scott, what if Doug insists on a meeting?"

"Take him to court. That's what the Goddamned lawyers are paid to do."

"It would take months and months to go through the courts. Maybe a year. And Jeremy may not have that much time."

Scott didn't say anything.

"Scott....Scott!"

Scott had put his pizza down, chin in hand. "Sorry, Faith. I was just thinking, we took that road, to Peoria, and met that SOB once, and I don't mean son of Beelzebub, and it didn't help matters. It put you in a tailspin of depression for about a month. I don't see why you'd even consider meeting him again."

"I'm not! In fact, I made it clear to Bill that this is what I don't want. And maybe it won't even come up. Bill says maybe we'll be lucky and he'll just turn over the records."

"I hope you're right, but I fear you're not. My guess is he'll refuse and play hardball. And Ludwig is just doing his job as a lawyer to let you know this creep may make outlandish demands and conditions. As a client, you have to be clear on what you will and will not do. Or give and not give. And I think meeting Doug is one of those things you should not do."

Faith's voice rose to a higher pitch. "I already told you, I don't want to."

"And you don't have to."

"I hope not."

He took a deep breath. "Okay, let's not argue about what hasn't happened yet. I have two positive suggestions. Do you want to hear them?"

"Sure."

"First, I'd be glad to go with you to meet with Bill Ludwig next time. I know you're sharp, but I deal with the legal eagles every week, so I know how they think."

"You're probably right. I'm not thinking with my brain. I'm feeling with my gut."

"And the second suggestion is to talk to Father Whitmore."

"To my father confessor?"

"Hey, my dad did the same thing, helping people through difficult times. And when you were haunted by Doug, he was a lifesaver."

"I guess you're right."

"There's nothing wrong with telling the good Father you're vulnerable. He'll help you."

"Yeah, why didn't I think of that?"

Later that evening when Scott and Faith went to bed, she snuggled close to him. She felt so lucky to have a good man with her to face this family problem. She didn't want to have trouble with Scott over meeting Doug. Faith was comfortable next to Scott, but she remembered the journal in her drawer that had helped her sort out problems. She was tempted to get up and write in the journal, but didn't want to wake Scott. As she drifted off to sleep she thought about what she would write about this new problem.

If she wrote something, the heading would be:

"Problem time."

On the next line would be:

"Doug."

CHAPTER 6

Faith had given Bill Ludwig her email address and asked him to let her know as soon as possible when he could meet with her. Several days after their initial meeting he sent a message saying he could see her the following Monday, and would have more specific suggestions. She forwarded the note to Scott and asked him for a good time he could go with her. He replied with, "As early as you can make it Monday." After she locked in a 9:30 appointment with the law firm's receptionist, she called Father Whitmore.

"Hello Father, it's Faith Armstrong."

"Hi, Faith. It's good to hear your voice. I missed you at church Sunday."

"Sorry, we had family in town last week."

"Maybe we'll see you this week."

"You can count on it."

"What's up?"

"As usual, I have a problem."

"Big problem?"

"Yes and no. In some ways not so big as what I've talked over with you in the past. But it's complicated and messy. And in some ways much more serious, because it's medical."

"You or Scott?"

"Not us, it's Jeremy."

"Can you drive over?"

"I hate to ask you for Friday afternoon, but I had to take Monday off and I'm behind the eight ball at the hotel."

"Friday afternoon? Uh...."

"Yeah. If that doesn't work for you...."

"Uh, well, it can work. I was going to spend the afternoon at the Art Institute and my wife was meeting me for an evening downtown. So, I could come early and we could have a long lunch."

"Fine. How about Berghoff's, one o'clock, and we'll miss the noon-to-one crowd."

It was settled.

～

Faith had gotten to know Fritz, one of Scott's favorite septuagenarian waiters. She made a reservation for an alcove in the back where she and Scott had their second meeting. That alcove was usually one of Fritz's tables. It had a special meaning for her because that's where Scott first displayed his charm and personality.

As soon as Faith left work to meet Father Whitmore she felt better, because she was sure he would help her see the matter more clearly. Faith arrived ten minutes early to make sure she got there first, and told the maître d' and Fritz to expect her guest.

"Well, Father, do I still call you 'Father' when you wear a tweed sport coat and jeans?"

"Call me whatever you like. Maybe Father Incognito would do."

"I appreciate you meeting me today. I know how busy you are."

"Just trying to soak up a little art and culture, so it was easy to come early and see you. Do you want to order before you tell me what's on your mind?"

Fritz appeared and made a few recommendations which they accepted, much to his satisfaction.

Faith's smile disappeared. "This is a double whammy. Last weekend Jeremy and his family came to Oak Park, and he has kidney problems."

"How bad?"

"Too soon to tell. They're still trying to diagnose it. Well, that's one whammy. And to find out if this might be a hereditary condition, the doctors need medical histories. So, the other whammy is that I had to tell Jeremy and the whole family about Doug."

He shook his head. "That's tough."

"It was hard, but the worst part is that this week I've been working with my lawyers to figure out how to persuade or force Doug to hand over his family medical records."

"You haven't contacted him yet?"

"No. And I don't want to contact him myself. But the lawyers aren't sure I can stay in the background. And Scott doesn't want me to get involved with Doug. I respect that, because he was the one who helped me locate Doug and even met the creep while I watched him from the safety of the car."

"So, more problems?"

"Well, it's just so messy and convoluted. Doug doesn't even know he's the father of the twins, so asking him for his medical records to help his son, or sons, is not simple. He can just ignore us and we'll have to prove paternity, but to do that we'll have to get his DNA, and if he refuses to provide a sample, we'll have to provide witnesses or some kind of reasonable proof that he is the twins' father."

"That is a mess, indeed."

"Yeah, and I guess this is the point where I should break down and cry, but emotionally I'm too afraid."

"Afraid?"

"Uh-huh. Afraid of Jeremy having kidney failure. Well, if it's hereditary, it could affect Jon, too. And maybe the kids. I'm afraid it might wreck the family. And I'm scared of what will happen if we are forced to deal directly with Doug. If he doesn't hand over the medical files, the doctors can't do a thorough check of the hereditary angle. And if Doug causes a stink, then getting involved with him might cause problems in the family."

"What does Scott think about this?"

"Scott is an angel. He's the one who insisted I see you. His words were something like 'Tell him you're vulnerable.'"

And it's true. Usually I'm in control, but all of this is out of my hands. I don't know what to do. There's not much I can do."

"Well, at least you've got Scott's support."

"Hmm. Half way, I'd say. He's an angel, but he's against me meeting Doug. I told him I'd do anything to get the records. We had a kind of argument about that. All I can be sure of is that if we need to tangle directly with Doug, it may be rough for Scott and me."

"Sounds like you have at least a triple whammy. How can I help you?"

"You're my confessor, and my first confession is that I'm vulnerable. Next, I guess just listen to me ramble and not make a fool of myself. For so many years I was in control, and by myself. Now that I'm so tied up with my family, and not in control, I feel helpless."

"Okay, the first thing I can tell you is that at some time we're all helpless. We can't control the weather. We can't control our health. We can't control other people. So you may have thought you were in charge of things in the past, but that was an illusion. Recognizing that you're helpless shouldn't be a guilt trip. It's just an act of reality adjustment."

"Hearing that from you does make me feel better."

"What are you going to do?"

"I don't know, Father. Monday the lawyer will make his suggestions. He's looking over our detective report on Doug, figuring out the best strategy."

"What would you like to do?"

"Just have the lawyer handle it, let him ask Doug for the information, and hopefully he'll hand over the papers."

Her priest tilted his head back and forth. "Not very likely, huh?"

"No, it'll probably be a lengthy negotiation between his lawyer and our lawyer."

"I see what you mean. It's complex and indirect."

"Yeah. And I like simple and direct. When I'm in control that's what I insist on. When I'm not in control, I'm out of control."

"Alright. Now your confessor changes to priest-gadfly. How do you feel about Doug?"

"Feel?"

"Yes, feel or think about him."

"I've already told you, I'm afraid of him."

"Bad dreams?"

"Not like before. He's not haunting me. But he's there, and I'm vaguely aware of him when I wake up."

"Okay, let me try the direct approach. Have you forgiven him?"

"No. I told you, I never blamed him for my getting pregnant when I was younger. What I resented when I saw him again a year ago was that he's still a testosterone letch."

"And you haven't forgiven him for being a letch."

"No. Should I?"

"I don't know, Faith. He wronged you, and you resent it. And you've got to deal with him. Directly or indirectly. I just thought it'd be easier for you to handle all this if you didn't have the extra burden of anger and resentment."

"You're probably right. I'll work on it. I thought I'd never forgive Dad, but it worked out. That took time, so this will take time, too."

"Right. Forgiveness is a process. The important thing is to start the process."

"Father, You're absolutely right. Why couldn't I see it myself? The fact that I'm so mad at Doug is what makes this situation so difficult. Ironically, that's the one thing I can control, and haven't tended to."

"There's never a better time than the present. The past is gone, but the beginning of the future is now."

"I said Scott is an angel. So you must be a saint."

"Well, my child, I checked in the mirror before coming today, and haven't sprouted wings yet. But do you mind if we close with a prayer today?"

"Of course not. I need it."

"Our Father in Heaven, hear our prayers. We are weak. Helpless. Broken. We ask that you strengthen us, come to our aid, mend us. We offer our thanks for your support in the past, and we pledge our faith in coming difficulties. We trust your power to heal and make us whole. We ask forgiveness for our shortcomings and for the salvation of all people. And we pray for your help in forgiving others. This we pray in Jesus' name. Amen."

Faith went back to work, her batteries recharged, her spirit uplifted, and her mind set on initiating the process of forgiveness for Doug.

CHAPTER 7

Faith said, "Thanks Scott, for insisting that I see Father Whitmore."

"I knew it was the right thing to do. When you're a preacher's kid, there are some things you learn about church and men of the cloth. Well, I guess these days you could say women of the cloth, too. Anyway, the most important thing is that the most important stuff doesn't happen on Sunday. It's when people are hurting. Marriage problems, kid problems, business and financial difficulties, sickness, and the biggest biggie, death. That's when the reverend earns his or her money. These things don't wait for the weekend or the holy day of the week."

"Say, you sound like a preacher yourself."

He laughed. "Do I hear myself becoming my father?"

"I never knew him, but it sounds like a compliment for you to go from preacher's kid to preacher."

They had a nice weekend, and patched up their differences over the possibility of Faith meeting Doug. They were ready, a united front for seeing Bill Ludwig Monday morning.

"COME IN, come in, Faith. And this must be Scott, the star Trib reporter I've heard so much about."

"Bill, he's the best thing that ever happened to me."

Scott said, "As a reporter, I'll leave those flattering comments off the record. But let me say I appreciate what you've done, and what you're doing. We thought it was best for both of us to meet you this time, because the options for handling this seem open-ended, and it's more efficient if we can hear the options together and help fine tune them so we can move ahead. Speed is important."

"Alright, Scott, glad to have you aboard with our team. Let me say, before I forget, that you two did an excellent piece of research/detective work when you located Douglas G. Parnelli and not only placed him geographically, but also financially and personally. Now what I want to do first is to lay out a picture of Mr. Parnelli, and then his lawyer."

Faith flinched. "You contacted his lawyer?"

"No, no, no! Of course not. Nothing without discussing it with you first. But we have our own research department. Douglas G. Parnelli is our adversary, and you've helped us size him up. He'll come as a team with a lawyer, so how we approach him depends partly on who he brings to the table with him. You already know most of what we have on Doug, so I'll just give a quick overview of how we see him.

"Parnelli is a typical downstate small businessman. Graduated from WIU with a business major. Right after graduation he went into the family contracting business, and that's all he's ever done. Strictly a small potato, no major legal background. More about that later. And as you and your detective partner know, he's a real lover boy, with two marriages shipwrecked, and a number of affairs. We only had legal affairs researched in Peoria County. He and his company sued a couple of deadbeats for nonpayment of some building projects. A few people sued his company for bad construction work.

"Next his lawyer. Same lawyer represented Parnelli Construction in suits they filed and when they got sued. Stanley S. Simon, classmate of Parnelli, same fraternity. Law school at U of I, worked for a small law firm in Peoria for five years, then opened his own one-man office. Only has a receptionist. Does wills, some small business clients. Strictly small time.

"Uh, sorry. Got ahead of myself. Should have started out today saying I had a three-act performance: first, information, which I just gave you. Second, a strategy suggestion. And third, question/answer session. Well, we could have question/answer at any time, but what do you think?"

Faith said, "Go ahead with your suggestions."

"Righto. Based on our profile of Parnelli and Simon, what we find is a small town businessman and a small-time lawyer. Therefore, we suggest a simple, straightforward request for the medical records, avoiding any threatening language or adversarial tactics. Parnelli and his lawyer will probably posture and object, but eventually they should accept our request for the papers in exchange for a stipulation of no responsibility, no financial obligation on the part of Parnelli."

Scott spoke up. "You'd make that binding on both parties, wouldn't you?"

Bill Ludwig smiled. "You're as sharp as I thought. Sure. But we don't want to stipulate it up front. We want his side to make the request, and we'll just go along with it, making it a mutual agreement of no responsibility, no obligation for either party."

Scott returned the smile. "Good."

Faith asked, "How would you get this to Doug?"

"Certified registered mail. Overnight. We go directly to him, don't mention his lawyer."

"I see. And how would you word it?"

"Here's a draft, copies for each of you. Read it over, and we can make changes if needed."

Dear Mr. Parnelli:

Our firm has been hired to represent a woman with whom you fathered a child some thirty years ago. Now that child, as an adult, has developed medical problems and the person's physician has requested maternal and paternal medical records, especially such details as cause of death, age at time of death, and any kidney/renal problems of living family members. The physician also requests the same information for each parent's (our client's and your) parents and their siblings.

Our only concern is the present and future health of this person. Any past or future medical treatment will be borne by this person. We trust you will share our concern for the health of this person and will promptly provide medical records using the enclosed forms (which may be copied as needed). The forms can be returned in the enclosed prepaid overnight mailer.

Thank you for your speedy consideration of this matter.

FAITH LOOKED RELIEVED. "Well written. It's simple and straightforward, non-threatening and non-adversarial." She turned to Scott.

"Looks good. That's the shot across the bow, so to speak. Then you do the serious negotiating with what Parnelli and his lawyer say in reply."

"Yes. We try to anticipate as much as possible. He'd be a fool to just hand over medical records without some safeguards and protections, and that's what we start negotiating on the next round."

Faith frowned. "How much time will this take?"

"We never know. Depends on the individual. And the attorney."

Faith glanced at Scott, who nodded. "Sure, send it out. It's a simple, non-offensive request. The tough negotiating and name-calling can be taken up later."

"Good, folks. I'll have the letter out in this afternoon's mail."

CHAPTER 8

ill Ludwig prided himself on being an efficient and productive lawyer, bringing in lots of client-hours for the firm, and getting good results. He always did his homework well in advance.

As soon as he sent off the letter to Doug, he prepped the receptionist with instructions. "If Parnelli or his lawyer calls, probably Stanley Simon, tell him I'm on the phone. And on this legal pad I've written down a script for you to follow when you talk to Simon."

Bill kept Friday afternoons free, because he liked to clean up odds and ends from the previous week, and get ready for the next. He had hoped to hear from Parnelli by Friday, so he could talk to Faith before the weekend. But these things took time, and he wasn't surprised that he had received no call. He was patient. He had to wait for the Parnelli team to make its move.

At 2:40 Friday afternoon he was getting a cup of coffee in the outer office when the call came through. The receptionist waved him over. "Mr. Simon? Representing Mr. Parnelli?"

Bill moved next to the secretary and pointed to the script on the legal pad with the tip of his ball point pen.

"Could you spell your name for me? Yes. S-i-m-o-n. Yes, Mr.

Simmon, you wanted to talk to Mr. Ludwig? What? Not Simmon, but Simon? Was that one m or two m's? Oh, yes, one m. Yes. Mr. Ludwig is on the phone now."

Bill moved his pen to another line of the script.

"How long will you be available this afternoon? Alright, I'll see if he can return your call in the next hour or two."

When she hung up, he said nothing, just flashed a smile, gave her a pat on the shoulder, and formed a perfect circle with his index finger and thumb.

Fifteen minutes later he emerged from his office, poured a half cup of coffee, and said, "Okay, you can call Simon now," and pointed to the bottom of the legal pad.

"Hello, is this the office of Mr. Stanley Simon? Oh! This is Mr. Simon? I'm sorry, but when you called you asked to speak to Mr. Ludwig, well, actually, we have two Mr. Ludwigs, father and son. Winston Ludwig is the son. William Ludwig is the father, a senior partner and one of the founding partners in the firm....Yes, I thought you meant the senior partner. I think he's off the phone now. Please wait while I connect you."

Bill Ludwig was seated behind his huge walnut desk, the Armstrong-Parnelli file to his left, his coffee cup on a coaster to the right. Sandwiched in between was a legal pad anchored to the desk by an Italian glass paperweight. His receptionist rang. "Mr. Simon is on the line."

"Yes, I'll be right with him." He picked up his coffee cup and took a sip, watching the second hand of his desk clock make a quarter of a circuit. He cleared his throat and then answered the phone with a friendly voice.

"Yes, Mr. Simon. Bill Ludwig here. Sorry to keep you waiting. You know how it is, Friday afternoon, trying to clean things up and get out of the Loop before the rush hour. How can I help you today?"

A squeaky voice answered. "Stanley Simon here. I'm calling for Douglas Parnelli. He hired me to represent him. You sent him a request for family medical records."

"Sure. I remember it. Simple request. All we need is the medical records. Nothing else. No need for any fancy legal procedures. Could have been handled without any of us law jockeys interfering, but my client asked me to write the letter, and I'm on retainer, so I just sent the letter directly to Mr. Parnelli. If Mr. Parnelli prefers to have you handle the matter, that's fine."

"Since your client chose to have legal representation, my client thought it would be better to have representation, too."

"Fine. That's his choice. And I suppose he has empowered you to act for him?"

"Yes."

"Good. Is he prepared to send the medical info? Any questions? The medical forms were provided by the physician who needs the family background to see if there's a hereditary predisposition for kidney/renal problems."

"Uh, before we get into the forms themselves, let's get back to home plate."

"Okay. What's on your mind?"

"Well, to begin with, just why do you think my client should provide these records?"

"Stanley—can I call you Stanley?"

"Yeah. Sure."

"Stanley, we're trying to keep this as simple as possible, put clients in front and lawyers in back. So that's why we drafted the letter as a simple request. Actually, we're asking for a favor. If your client would just be good enough to provide the records, we'll go away and not bother him again."

"And why would he do that? He doesn't have to."

"No. You're right. He doesn't have to. We didn't say he had to. Or that we would force him to. It would be easier for everyone and a lot quicker if he handed over the records so that the doctor can proceed with his diagnosis. I think you understand that we're not discussing some legal nicety that can wait for months or years of negotiation and litigation. We're talking about the health, the life, of a human being."

"Well, just a minute. You know as well as I do that providing these records would admit, or at least imply, paternity."

"Stanley, let me put you and Mr. Parnelli at ease. We're not interested in the least in a paternity suit, if that's what you're getting at. This child we're talking about is now an adult, so child support isn't a concern."

"And how do you know Mr. Parnelli is actually the father of this child?"

"Very simple. My client was young and inexperienced when she met Mr. Parnelli. She had relations with him once, her first time, and with no one else, and she got pregnant."

"Is that all you have? The word of one woman thirty years after the fact?"

"I've known this woman a long time. She's a responsible, trustworthy professional. Her story will stand up."

"Not in court."

"I'm not talking about court."

"And how do you think you're going to persuade me to persuade Mr. Parnelli it's in his best interest to provide his family medical records to an unknown person for unknown reasons?"

"I can understand you want to serve the interests of your client the same as I'm serving the interests of my client. That's why I said, to begin with, that this is a request, a favor we're asking for, in the interest of a person whose health, maybe life, is in question."

"And how do we know that?"

"Would you like a formal statement of medical condition from the doctor? We'd be glad to provide that."

"Well, that would help. I mean, I don't know what Mr. Parnelli will say, but I can't advise him to fork over his medical data without some thirdparty verification. I mean, other than this woman and you."

"Fine. I understand, Stanley. I'll arrange for that to be sent. I have a copy in my client's file, and can fax it to you. To you or to Mr. Parnelli? Would that be sufficient?"

"Just a minute. The matter can't be settled just with a doctor's statement. We still haven't taken care of the paternity question. And this mystery woman. Who is she?"

"You can understand why she doesn't want to come forward. That teenage pregnancy was traumatic for her. After his one-night stand, Mr. Parnelli went back to college, graduated, had a family, entered the family business. My client had a much tougher time as a single parent, and doesn't want to relive it."

"Uh...sounds like you know a lot about my client."

"Our firm tries to do its research. Homework."

"So you're aware of Parnelli Construction Company?"

"Yes. It's a matter of public record."

"And you're not interested in any action against the company? I have represented both Parnelli personally and his company."

"Heavens, no! Is that what's holding you and your client back?"

"I'd like to see that in writing."

"We said in our letter that all we wanted was the medical records. That's already stated, so what more do you want?"

"A signed statement that you and your client will hold neither Mr. Parnelli personally nor Parnelli Construction Company legally or financially responsible for this woman or her offspring."

"In exchange for the medical records?"

"I could advise my client to consider that. It would protect his interests, as you said."

"Fine. I'm sure my client will agree to that, because I already explored that with her. Mind you, she didn't bring it up, but as her attorney I had to ask her if she wanted me to make any claims, financial or otherwise on Mr. Parnelli, and she assured me she is only interested in the welfare of her child. Her concern is purely medical, not monetary. So I can draw up an agreement to that effect. Of course, you will understand that if my client is going to forego any legal/financial claim on your client, that we'd make this a mutually binding clause."

"Sure. Naturally."

"My client wants to go forward on this, so I can fax you a draft of the text yet this afternoon, and send the original by mail to reach you by Monday. My client has empowered me to act as her agent in this matter."

"Okay."

"It's a standard formula: I'll draw it up to protect both clients: Both parties agree to not hold the other party liable for any legal or financial obligations."

"Yeah. Something like that."

"And you can recommend your client to provide medical records, given that stipulation?"

"I can't guarantee it. We'd probably still want to know who this woman is, and details of the pregnancy."

"I was hoping you wouldn't raise that."

"And why not?"

"Well, it's embarrassing for everyone. My client would have to relive an unfortunate teenage pregnancy."

"So?"

"And your client would have to admit that, as an adult, he was twenty-one at the time, he seduced and impregnated a sixteen year old."

"He's not admitting to that."

"And we're not asking him to. But by pushing the identity matter, he forces a private matter into the public arena. Makes something painless into something painful."

"Painless?"

"Yes. If he hands over the records, we say good-by, and that's the end of it. Painless. He doesn't have to admit he had sex with a minor, which would seem to be a painful admission."

"And if we don't?"

"Don't what?"

"Don't hand over the medical info."

"Well, you can see how the scales tip in favor of my client. Experienced college man seduces inexperienced high school girl."

"That's one reason why my client may not want to do anything. He doesn't want all this spread around."

"Now we're on the same track. We want to keep this quiet. If he gives us the records, no one knows about all this. If he doesn't, that's when it all becomes public."

"You still don't have any proof."

"Well, Stanley, you know, I didn't want to put this to you, but did you ask your client if he had sexual relations with a woman thirty years ago and might have got her pregnant?"

"That's privileged information, and you know it. He doesn't have to say anything about his sexual history. But at least tell me where this...meeting took place."

"Ask him if he had intimate relations with a high school girl thirty years ago."

"Where?"

"This would be a girl in Canton, if he has trouble remembering which one. My client only had one such experience, so she remembers it well."

"I'll ask him."

"Please do. I have the doctor's statement in my file and will fax it with the no-liability stipulation."

"Okay."

"The only thing I'd add is that we both know legal matters are notorious, infamous, for delays. But medical conditions don't accept any delays or extensions. Can I expect a reply from you by midweek?"

"I'll do my best."

"I'd appreciate that, Stanley. Good talking to you."

It only took Bill a few minutes to modify the stipulation text on his computer file and print it out. He handed it to the receptionist with the doctor's statement, blocking out Jeremy's name, and jotted down Simon's fax number. "Send this right away."

He started back into his office and turned around. "Great performance on the phone. Bravo." He clapped his hands in appreciation before he shut his door.

"Hi, Faith, Bill Ludwig here. Got a minute?"

"Sure, Bill. Any news?"

"First contact, not from Parnelli, but his lawyer."

"And?"

"We played a little cat-and-mouse. I asked him to keep it simple and do us a favor by just sending the records. He wanted protection for his client, so we agreed to a stipulation of no liability for him. And, like Scott suggested, we made it a mutually binding agreement for both parties. I just faxed him that agreement and the doctor's statement, and pushed him for a mid-week reply."

"And?"

"He said he'd do his best."

"So we've got to wait a while."

"Uh-huh. I used the medical button, telling him this kidney condition won't wait for legal delays."

"Well, that's as much as we could expect, on the first contact."

"Yes. We never thought he'd roll over and play dead, and say 'Take whatever you want.'"

"No, I guess not."

"Faith, the worst we could have feared is, his lawyer would call and tell us to go to Hell and sue from there."

"Then we'd be in a Hell of a fix."

There was a pause, and then Bill realized she was joking. "Yeah, that's good, Faith. Hell of a fix." Well, pass on the news to Scott, and I'll contact you as soon as I hear something. I know you thought this was a simple request. And it is. But like I reminded you, the devil is in the details."

PART II
THE DEVIL IN THE DETAILS

CHAPTER 9

*W*hile eating a late supper in the condo, Scott and Faith talked over the latest legal wrinkle.

"I'll grant you this much, Faith, your lawyers are good. They were honest, up front that it was complicated and would take time. They made use of our detective work and backed it up with solid research. Their strategy is sound and their tactics are skillful."

"You think we're okay?"

"The only problem, dear, is you've got two unknowns, two variables, that neither we nor your lawyer can second guess."

"Parnelli and his lawyer?"

"Yes."

"So what do we do?"

"Wait. Hope. Pray."

"And then?"

"We do what we have to do."

Faith asked, "Anything?"

"No! Not just anything. We do what we have to."

"I hope we don't have to do whatever has to be done, just let the lawyers take care of it. Scott, I don't want to meet Doug. Just seeing him was enough for me."

"You don't have to. And that's what we need to make clear to Bill and this other lawyer."

"We did make it clear we didn't want to have any direct contact with him."

"Then you don't have to."

"I sure hope so."

Their discussion was interrupted by a call from Jeremy. The clan had never met in Springfield, and Melanie had been trying to get the whole family to come downstate. Jon was free the next weekend, and Jeremy hoped Scott and Faith could make it. Scott said he could work late Friday and they could leave mid-morning Saturday.

There was no new development in Jeremy's condition.

Faith looked forward to a weekend out of Chicago.

THURSDAY AFTERNOON BILL LUDWIG got a call from Stanley Simon, which he took immediately.

"Hi, Stanley, thanks for getting back to me so soon."

"Hi, Bill. I got the doctor's statement and the no-liability stipulation. That part looks good."

"So where are we?"

"Parnelli still is leery about handing over papers to an unknown person. After all, this woman never even told Doug she was pregnant. And then she didn't contact him for thirty years. So this comes as a surprise."

"No, she didn't contact Mr. Parnelli. Nor did Mr. Parnelli come back to see if his moments of pleasure had resulted in pregnancy. She endured nine months of a humiliating pregnancy, interrupting her high school education, and not once during that time did Mr. Parnelli make any contact with her. She didn't bother him through the years for anything, financial or emotional support, and wouldn't do so now, if she had a choice. However, this is not elective, it's a necessity."

"Maybe it's a necessity for your client, but we'd like to make it clear that whatever my client does, it's elective for him. You've shown no proof that he's the father of this child."

"So is he denying the possibility that this child is his?"

"He's not required to prove that he's not this person's father. There's lots of fatherless kids in the world, but he's not obligated to prove he's not the father of any of them."

"Does he deny he ever had sexual relations with a Canton high school girl while he was a student at Western Illinois?"

"Conversations between my client and myself are privileged. So I don't have to answer that. What I can tell you is that Mr. Parnelli is a respectable citizen of Peoria, a respected business man. He is a tax-paying, law-abiding man and is responsible for his actions."

"He is responsible?"

"Yes."

"Responsible for what?" Bill's voice had shifted from a conversational tone to an interrogation mode.

"Well...for his family."

"His family?"

"Yes."

"Which one?"

"What do you mean?"

"Do you mean his family with Colleen? Or his family with Chanelle?"

"Well, you fancy Chicago lawyers do your research. Sure, he's been married twice. But he takes care of his kids."

Ludwig said, "Yeah. His kids. By both wives. Pays alimony to the wives and child support for the kids. He's responsible."

"That's right! He takes care of his responsibilities."

"Any other responsibilities he takes care of?"

"Uh, yes, he runs his business, has a solid reputation as a contractor."

"We'll leave the business out of this. Any other responsibilities?"

"Like what?"

"Family responsibilities."

"I already told you, he's been married twice, and takes care of these two families."

"So he has just the three kids, two by the first wife and one by the second?"

"What do his children have to do with it?"

"You said he's responsible for his family, families. And his children. So he has just the three children?"

"Like you said about his company, it's a matter of public record."

"Well, yes, business ownership, marriages, divorces, yes. But not other arrangements. Does he have any children with his common law live-in Shirley?"

"That's none of your Goddamn business!"

"I beg to differ, counselor. When you make a claim that your client is responsible, and takes care of his children, we expect that you'll keep track of how many children there are. Both within and outside the formalities of marriage. Should I ask how many other offspring are waiting in the wings?"

"No, you shouldn't. Because I don't think my client would be pleased to hear any questions like that. If you want to persuade him to do you a favor, you could try to be nice."

Bill shifted to a pleasant tone. "Mr. Simon, I can be nice as pie. I'd rather use honey than vinegar. But I have a point to make here. If we were in a court of law, and the judge asked relevancy, I'd say that Mr. Parnelli is responsible to his legitimate offspring, and possibly also for one or more illegitimate children, providing financial support and the like, but for my client he appears unwilling to offer a medical record that costs him nothing!"

"Alright, let's get right down to it. You're the fancy Chicago lawyer in a big skyscraper firm and you have a hot shot research team and a lot of information on my client. But I have the client, and he has the records. So you may have to dance to our hick town tune. And he may not hand over the records unless he has a face-to-face with your client."

"Stanley, Stanley. Let's back off a minute and look at this again, as gentlemen. I respect any lawyer, whether he, or she, is on Wall

Street, Michigan Avenue, or Back Alley. Big firm or one-person office. Now. All we're asking for is medical records. No admission of paternity, no financial claim, no obligation whatsoever. And we've supplied the physician's statement backing up our assertion of medical necessity along with the no-liability stipulation. We've come a long way in this. If I got a little testy a few minutes ago, it's because I have a person's health in mind. And that's why we want to get this settled as expeditiously as possible."

"And so far you have no agreement from my client. Zilch! So you talk to your client and see if she wants to get the papers from my client. He may consider that kind of arrangement. And then again he may not. I don't know what I'll recommend to him. But that's one of his conditions. Well, I have a client waiting. It's been nice talking to you."

"Yes, Stanley, good talking to you. Let me suggest—"

"Sorry, I gotta go."

Bill Ludwig hung up the phone. He covered his face with his hands. His baritone voice descended to a gravely bass. "GOD-DAMMIT! Goddamn Stanley Simon, Douglas G. Parnelli, Bill Ludwig, the entire world, and its complete population of dogs and cats and all their fleas."

CHAPTER 10

*B*ill Ludwig went to the men's room. On the way back he eyed the coffee. His receptionist said, "Mr. Ludwig, you're already over your limit."

"Okay, I'll make it a half cup." He poured his half dose of caffeine and went back in his office. He sipped it slowly, to make it last, watching the clock hands move from 3:45 to 3:55. Reluctantly he picked up the phone.

"Faith. It's Bill Ludwig. Do you have time for an update?"

"Sure. Shoot."

"Parnelli's lawyer called a little while ago. There's good news and bad news.

"Give me the good news first."

"Alright. They're thinking about handing over the records. They haven't agreed to it, but the physician's statement and the no-liability stipulation seem to have satisfied them."

"And the downside?"

"Well...he wants to do the delivery of the records in person."

"The lawyer?"

"Parnelli."

There was a long pause. "Did you hear me, Faith? Parnelli wants to hand over the medical papers."

"I heard you. Hmm. And...he wants to give them to...you?"

"No."

"Oh, no, not...to me?"

"Right."

"Why?"

"I don't know. Simon dropped that on me just before he hung up. He wouldn't elaborate on it."

"You didn't make any suggestion yourself about the transfer of the papers?"

"Hell, no. He was singing his song about we didn't have any proof of paternity and anything his client did was non-compulsory, and I was pushing the angle about his responsibilities. Simon got a little hot, made the condition for the release of the papers a face-to-face meeting, and then hung up."

"Did you agree to that?"

"Of course not. I tried to tell him we should keep it as simple and uncomplicated as possible, but he wouldn't listen."

"What do we do now?"

"Well, think about it over the weekend, and we can regroup next week. I guess you and Scott need to talk it over before you see me."

"What are the options?"

"The black and white options are: accept his condition of a personal meeting and get the papers. Or refuse the condition and insist that he hand over the papers."

"What's your recommendation?"

"I leave that to you, but I can help you weigh the positive and negative of each option. You want speedy delivery, and a meeting should get you the documents quickly, at the cost of an unpleasant encounter with Parnelli. If we refuse his condition, we'd have to go to court to force him to provide the papers, which would take time. Maybe a year. And there's no guarantee we'd win. If we didn't win, that doesn't mean we could just go back to option one and say, 'Well, since we lost in court, we'll concede the point and meet with you.' In other words, taking option two probably burns the bridge to option one."

"Well, thanks for sorting it out. That gives us a clearer picture of our choices. Scott and I will discuss it and get back to you. Can we see you Tuesday morning at 9:30?"

"Sure. I'll set it up."

"Bill, do you have any idea why they want a personal meeting?"

"The only thing I can tell you is that it's Parnelli's idea, not the lawyer's. Makes no legal sense at all. If he was my client, I'd advise against it. Lawyers get paid to insulate people from each other. There's always the possibility for tension, friction, conflict, maybe worse, when people get together."

"So why does Parnelli want the meeting?"

"There's got to be a personal dimension to it. I don't like it, but you'll have to figure out if speedy delivery is worth the unpleasant meeting."

"I see. Well, we'll be in your office 9:30 Tuesday."

Faith slowly put the receiver down, missing the cradle and clunking it on the table, then picked it up and found its proper home. "Damn!" She was cursing not the phone, but the ghost from three decades ago who had haunted her and now bedeviled her with this unreasonable request. Bedeviled, yes. Even when he first appeared at Pappy's Pizza parlor, the waitresses had called him a devil. And now he was demanding to meet with her. But how do you prepare for a téte-a-téte with a devil? She didn't know and didn't want to find out.

Faith didn't want to discuss the matter on the phone with Scott. She called him to order and pick up a pizza on the way home, and was relieved she could leave a phone message, sure he'd check his messages before he left the office.

"Hi, hon. I got the usual, half sausage, half anchovies."

"Great."

Scott set the pizza down and gave her a peck. "Hey, what's wrong."

"Why do you think something's wrong?"

"Well, you had me get pizza, which means you don't want to cook, and the look on your face tells me you're not sure you want to eat."

"You read me like a newspaper. Bill Ludwig called me late afternoon."

She opened the pizza box as he got two beers out of the fridge.

"Trouble?"

"Possibly. The physician's request for the records and the statement of non-liability seemed to persuade them to fork over the medical info."

"That's good."

"Yeah, but they asked for personal delivery."

"Personal? Which person to which person?"

"It's not clear, but apparently it involves Doug and me."

"Details?"

"Not available. It seems that Ludwig and Simon got into an argument, and Simon made the condition of a personal handover, and hung up."

"Hmm. And what does the legal vulture recommend?"

"He's leaving it up to us. The two main options are: one, speedy transfer of the records if we agree to a meeting; two, rejecting their conditions and risking our chances in court, which would take a year or more, and if we lose, it probably would rule out the chance of later going back to the personal meeting."

"Hmm. What's your idea?"

"I don't like either option. I want Jeremy and his doctor to see the records right away, but don't like the prospect of meeting Doug to get them. On the other hand, a court battle would take a year or so, and Ludwig says there's no guarantee we'd win. If we lost, Parnelli and his lawyer could thumb their noses at us, and we'd never get the medical data."

"That's the either/or. Which way do you lean?"

"Well, Scott, I don't want to be in the same room with Doug, and I know you're opposed to it. But I don't see any other possibility. Help me figure this out. I want us to be together on this."

He gritted his teeth and squinted. "Well, I don't know...." He took a huge bite of pizza.

"Talk to me, Scott. You were great when I asked you to help me locate Doug. Now I need your help more than ever. Dealing with Doug."

"Alright. Straight talk. Ludwig laid out two opposite extremes. But you realize there's an infinite number of possibilities in between. Our side can set conditions, their side can set conditions. Simon can say he wants a chocolate malted milk shake at the meeting. We can specify where the meeting takes place. That's a subset of option one. What I mean is, setting the conditions."

"Uh-huh."

"But Faith, remember, once you start quibbling about how the meeting will occur, you concede the point that you agree to a meeting."

"I guess so. And option two?"

"You never played poker, did you?"

"No, why?"

"Parnelli and Simon may be bluffing. They say they won't give us the papers without a meeting. But notice that they're practically conceding that a meeting will take place and the papers will be handed over."

"Well, not exactly. Maybe I didn't tell it to you the way Bill told it to me. When Ludwig and Simon got into a hot argument, Simon was claiming our side has no proof of paternity, so they aren't required to do anything."

"What does that mean?"

"I guess it means that since they aren't obligated to give us the records, they may be tough about the conditions. And the way Simon put it to Ludwig was, his client would consider handing over the papers if we agree to a face-to-face, but there's no guarantee at this point. It's just something his client will consider."

"And why do you think Parnelli wants to meet you?"

"Bill said it's got to be Parnelli's suggestion, because it doesn't make sense legally. Lawyers like to work attorney to attorney and keep messy personal issues and people and their emotions out of the negotiations."

"He's a smart lawyer. And what do you think about why Parnelli wants to meet with you?"

"It doesn't make legal sense to Bill. And it doesn't make sense to me. Scott, I think you have a hunch. Let me in on what you're thinking. After all, you met him in Peoria, so you have an advantage over Bill and me."

"I'm not sure you'll like it, but here goes."

They had finished the pizza and Scott was making decaf coffee as they talked.

"Doug's smooth. He could sell refrigerators to Eskimos and furnaces in the Amazon. So he thinks he can handle, and benefit, from a meeting. What can that possibly be?"

"I have no idea. You're way ahead of me, so tell me."

"Ludwig knows there's no legal benefit, and we've ruled out financial gain, so what's left? I think Ludwig is onto something. It must be personal."

"Something personal?"

"Yes, Faith, and what could that personal benefit or gain or advantage be?"

"Scott, I told you, I honestly don't know."

"Well, I think he wants to somehow connect with you."

"Connect?"

"Yeah. He wants to show his charm, impress you, and who knows what more?"

"Scott! How could he be interested in me now? I may have had some power of attraction as a teenager, but now...I'm no spring chicken."

"Excuse me, Faith, but it doesn't have to do with your power of attraction. It's his power of persuasion. Maybe seduction. He's got to show he still has his macho magnetism. Come on, Faith, you saw his Casanova act in Peoria."

"Scott, I appreciate your display of...jealousy...but I think you're wrong. It's too farfetched."

"Well, do you agree with Ludwig and me that Parnelli's motives must be personal?"

"Sounds right to me. Only because there's no other obvious reason."

"Then you tell me what these personal motives could be."

"I confess there's no logical alternative to your explanation. And I hate to admit it, but you may be more in tune with his testosterone ego."

"Okay. Now let's come back to the options. Simon says they don't have to turn over the records. We, or I, say we don't have to agree to a meeting."

"But then how do we get the records?"

"We call his bluff, and say no meeting."

"And if he says no records?"

"We can deal with that at the time. There's nothing in the cards that says this is the last deal. We don't need to win every hand to win the game.

"Oh, Scott, I'm so tired. That's enough for tonight. I just want to make one thing clear. This shouldn't drive a wedge between us."

"No, honey, let's try to face this together."

SCOTT WAS tired from a hard day and went to bed early. Faith said she'd stay up for a while. She sat in her recliner for a while, looking down at the side table where she had kept her journal. She waited another fifteen minutes to make sure that Scott was asleep, then tiptoed back into the bedroom and slowly opened her underwear drawer and pulled out the pink journal, holding it against her chest as she walked back to the recliner.

After looking at a blank page for a while, she wrote:

"Dear Journal, I may need you again.

Good times. Yes, I couldn't be happier, with a great family, and Scott as a loving companion.

Bad times. The news of Jeremy's kidney condition, and maybe

for Jon and their children, is terrible, and there's nothing I can do about it.

Problem times. Scott and I get along well, but we are in a collision course on how to handle Doug and the medical records of his family. I don't want to go against Scott and lose him, but I have to think of Jeremy and his condition. Somehow we've got to get those records. If I have to meet Doug...."

SHE CLOSED THE JOURNAL, turned the lights off and gazed out at Lake Michigan, illuminated by a near full moon. She asked the lake for a sign. A few moments later a shooting star streaked across the sky. At the same instant she thought of talking to Father Whitmore. Yes, she'd call him tomorrow.

CHAPTER 11

Stanley Simon cut short his call to Bill Ludwig when he was blindsided by the question about Shirley's kid. He used the excuse of having a client to talk to. And actually, he did. He didn't even take his hand off the phone, immediately calling Doug.

"Parnelli Construction. Can we help you build a better future?"

"This is Stan Simon. Let me talk to Doug."

"Oh, Mr. Simon. He's on a construction site. Do you want his cell number?"

"I have it." He hung up and dialed.

"Yes?"

"Doug, this is Stan. I need to talk to you."

"Hey, I got problems here. We're doing a room addition, and the rebar for the slab didn't pass inspection. The guys didn't epoxy the rebar into the existing slab. I got two guys on overtime, so how about ten Monday morning?"

"We need to talk today."

"What about?"

"Well, for one thing, Shirley."

"Who?"

"Shirley. And her kid."

"What about her? Uh...them?"

"They came up in the phone conversation with the Chicago lawyer."

"Well...Hell's bells! Why did you mention them to him?"

"I didn't. He mentioned them to me."

"Stan, you're cutting out, and I've got to get back to these guys. They've got to fix the rebar so I can pass city inspection Monday morning. The customer's holding up the next payment until after the inspection. If you need to see me today, meet me at Shorty's, 6:30. We can have a B and B."

Stan tried to protest, but the line was dead.

Shorty's was a bar not far from Parnelli Construction, one of Doug's hangouts. B and B was shorthand for burger and beer, a specialty of Shorty's.

Stan called his wife to tell her he'd be late, worked around the office on some papers, and headed cross town to Shorty's. He arrived at 6:35, grabbed the last open booth, and ordered a coke. The bar stools were already full, and their occupants were more than half loaded with TGIF brews. Stan was all too familiar with the scene and the routine. The bar was dim and dingy, illuminated by an odd assortment of neon beer signs. The patrons were more lit up than their surroundings.

He didn't want to be trapped in the B and B slippery slope to an all-night drunk with Doug. Stan knew the script by heart. Doug's second B and B was two beers and no burger. Several times Stan had felt sorry for Doug and drank five or six beers with him. But not tonight.

It was after seven when Doug breezed in, his dress pants and white shirt stained with concrete and tar and other unidentified construction material. He waved to Stan and yelled to the waitress, "Susie! Two B and B's over here. Two Bud Lites and deluxe burgers."

"Only the burger for me," Stan shouted after him.

"Have a beer, Stan. It's Friday night."

"Doug, this isn't the Phi Gam house, and we're not in a chugalug contest."

"Loosen up, Stan. Have a brew." He went to the men's room, and when he got back, downed half of his bottle before talking to Stan.

"So you talked to that fancy lawyer?" He had a broad smirk on his face.

"Yeah, Doug, and I didn't appreciate him pulling the rug from under me by telling me about your kid with Shirley."

"Shirley, shitly. What's that got to do with anything?"

"I'm painting this picture of you as a reputable businessman, a responsible family man to your three children, and he cuts my legs off by telling me about your fourth offspring." Stan clenched his jaw.

Doug laughed, his beer belly bouncing. "Three, four, what's the difference? I never was good at math."

"A helluva lot of difference. Credibility. If that happened in court, a judge or jury would give you a low score on your kid-arithmetic and also decide in favor of the plaintiff."

Doug held up an empty bottle, waving it toward the waitress as a signal for another. "I thought you said we don't have to go to court."

"We don't. Not if you're going to give them the medical stuff. But if you don't, they'll drag you to court. And they'll drag in your families."

"You said we could always give them the records, even on the courthouse steps, a few minutes before the trial."

"Sure, we could. But there'd be a lot of filing and court expenses. And you already owe me a bundle."

"Hey, Stan, Fiji buddy. What do you think I was doing all afternoon? All day? Busting my ass, hustling up some bucks. This guy owes me five grand, and if we pass inspection and pour cement Monday, he should cough it up. Half of it's yours."

When Susie brought his Bud Lite, Doug tried to slip his left hand behind her fanny and untie her apron. Apparently accustomed to this maneuver, she moved as deftly as a tight end to slip away from him. "No, no, Dougie, hands to yourself. You need both hands for your baby bottle, beer baby."

Stan rolled his eyes and shook his head. "Don't you ever stop?"

Doug had already pointed the bottom of the bottle toward the ceiling and was intent on emptying it in record speed. "Can't blame a guy for trying. Anyway, what do we do about the court stuff?"

"Doug, I hate to press you, but I've carried you a long time. And if this goes to court, it'll be expensive. Big time. And part of it I'll have to see in advance. In this one, you don't save any money. You don't avoid a judgment against you, and you can't make any money, even if you win you don't see any payment. Every dime of expense for this case goes down a rat hole. And some of the court costs are up front."

"No problem. You know I'm good for it. But tell me about the lawyer talk. Did you set up the meeting?"

"Well, I told them about it."

"And they bought it?"

"He needs to talk to his client. He didn't like it."

Doug ordered another B and B, a double beer minus the burger.

Susie stood behind Stan when she brought the beers, apparently preempting Doug's roaming hands. She tilted her head toward the bar. "Bill says this makes four, so two more, and that's all for you. Not like the other night. We're not running a Bud Lite taxi service."

Stan's chest heaved. "And what's that about?"

"Oh, last week they thought I had too much, and wouldn't let me drive home."

"Good for them."

Doug handed the second bottle to Stan.

"No, Stan, not tonight. I gotta get home."

"One more beer, at least.

"Okay, but that's it. I'm not on a binge with you tonight."

"Sure. I hate to drink alone."

"Then don't."

"Don't what?"

"Don't drink alone....Don't drink."

"Hey, I'm a changed man."

"The only change I've noticed is the switch from Bud to Bud Lite."

"Naw. Since I got saved, I'm a different person. Ask anyone at work."

"Right now I'm more concerned with this legal deal. And I have to tell you again, this meeting you want is crazy."

"You said it'd be safe with that paper about no liability."

"I said it should be safe. But it could backfire. And you can't give me any good reason for the meeting. You've got nothing to gain and a lot to lose."

"Hell, man, I've already lost everything. Well, except for my business. Lost two wives, two houses, three kids. Both of my wives are remarried, and they've turned the kids against me. Even Shirley moved away, so my youngest, too, was taken away from me."

"Doug, I didn't like the lawyer surprising me with Shirley's boy, but handled it. Well, right now let's stick to the meeting. Even if you have a face to face with this Canton gal, what would that get you? You'd still have two ex-wives, two former houses, three alienated children, and one departed live-in and her baby. And on top of that, an old girlfriend who you forced to meet you. It doesn't change a Goddamn thing."

"You don't get it, Stan, do you?"

"No, I don't, and neither does their lawyer. I hung up on him before he could ask again why you want a meeting, because I couldn't give him any good reason. So you tell me. I don't get it, and you need to educate me."

Doug put his bottle down and held both palms together. "It's about me. I've changed. Maybe you don't see it, but it's true. Well, trying to change. I've done a lot of shady things in my life, things I'm not proud of. My family life's a disaster, and even living with Shirley was a mistake. So for once in my life, I want to do something right with a woman. Meet her, tell her I'm sorry for messing up her life, try to make things better for her. And I catch hell for trying to be a nice guy, for once."

"Doug, get real. This woman was pregnant for nine months, had to drop out of high school, and it sounds like this fling with you wrecked her life. For thirty years she didn't bother you, and the only reason she contacts you now is for medical records to help her grown kid. Now what kind of comfort and warm feelings do you think your mug is going to bring her?"

"Okay, so it's about me."

"Yeah, Doug, it always seems to be about you."

"Right. I'd ask her to forgive me for getting her pregnant."

"I think the statute of limitations on forgiveness ran out a long time ago."

"Not according to the church people I've been talking to. It's never too late for forgiveness."

"Alright, Doug, I'm going to stop being your lawyer for a minute, and ask you a different question. Do you think your forgiveness is more important than this person's, your child's, health, and are you willing to hold back the medical records to satisfy your own guilt trip?"

Doug raised his head, his chin stuck out and his lower lip showing pink. "Is that you, Stan? I thought you were my lawyer."

Stan leaned back in his chair. "I said I'd put on a different hat for a minute, not a lawyer's hat, but a real human being's hat. Now I'm talking as your friend, asking you to do the right thing."

"Hey, that's not fair. I never said I wasn't going to give the medical stuff. It's not an either-or situation. This gal can have my family history, and I can have my meeting with her. So what's so wrong about that?"

"Let me give you a one-two-three, win-win-win solution. First, you give her the family medical records. That makes her happy, which is what you want. Second, by giving her the records now, you avoid more legal costs, which is a real plus for you. Third, you avoid any court battle, and given your past divorce scars and construction contract hassles, I think you'd be much better off spending your time here at Shorty's than in some court room."

"And why do you think I'm here so much? I go home to an empty apartment, no one to eat with, nobody to talk to."

"Sorry, buddy. But let me put on my lawyer's cap again. The best thing for you to do is to supply the medical records, drop the whole thing, and move on. Solve your personal and spiritual problems at church, not in a lawyer's office or in court. Of course, if you insist on pushing it, the meeting, then I'll push it. Against my better judgment. But it's gonna cost you. And you've run up such a bill with me already, that I'll have to take you up on that $2500 Monday."

"I'll get the check Monday. It'll take a few days to deposit and clear the check."

"Okay. $2500 sometime next week. And let me pass on the advice we learned in law school: never stiff your lawyer."

"Stan, we go way back. Let me buy you another beer. It's early. You've already missed supper with your family."

"Doug, I told you, I want to get home. I'll let you know when I receive some kind of word from the Chicago attorney."

"Just one more beer."

"You can drink it for me."

Stan got up and left, as Doug yelled for Susie, raising his empty bottle.

CHAPTER 12

aith and Scott were a little on edge about the Tuesday meeting, still not knowing how to face Ludwig. But they looked forward to the family weekend in Springfield. They had put their heads together and agreed to hold a family council at Jeremy and Melanie's house Saturday night.

They were rather quiet driving to the state capitol Saturday morning. As soon as they arrived at Jeremy and Melanie's, the juvenile fireworks went off. Jon and his family had beat them there, and the kids went wild. "Grandpa Scott and Grandma Faith, Grandpa Scott and Grandma Faith." When the pandemonium died down, Mark put the kids' question to Grandpa: "Are we gonna do a newspaper?"

Scott looked at Jeremy.

"Gee, I don't have all the computer gadgets that Jon does. I don't know how we'd do it."

Little Jeb had been following the rug rat pack around, dragging a Fisher-Price version of a battery powered karaoke set. Scott got down on the floor and asked Jeb, "Can we use this?"

Jeb dropped it in Scott's lap, glad to be the center of attention.

Stepping back from the kids a little, Scott assumed his broadcasting voice. Speaking into the kid karaoke device, he answered Mark's question: "Ladies and gentlemen. You are the first to hear an important announcement from the Armstrong Newspaper Company. We have just acquired radio broadcasting rights for our media organization."

"What's radio?" Mark asked.

"It's television without the picture," Scott said.

"Can you still see it?"

"No, you hear it."

Using again his professional announcer's delivery, he continued, "The Armstrong News Network is proud to open the first broadcast, after lunch, of station WARM, the warm station with the cool news. So stay tuned for the premiere broadcast."

Mark didn't quite get the point. "So we're not gonna do a newspaper?"

"No, kiddies, we're gonna do something better. We're gonna do a radio broadcast."

That spark ignited the fireworks again. "We're gonna do a radio broadcast, we're gonna do a radio broadcast."

Scott assigned reporters to cover the food and other news of the day.

After lunch, Scott started the broadcast, ticking off the reporters and their special news. Then he passed the Fisher-Price microphone to Beth. "And now we hear from our Springfield reporter, Beth Goodman, with news of our lunch."

Beth stood in front of the group, giggling, while the kids yelled, "Talk! Talk!"

Scott helped her out, raising the microphone up to her mouth. "We have experienced a slight delay due to technical difficulties. Now we bring you Beth Goodman."

Beth reported on what she had rehearsed with Scott. "We had a turkey today. Its head was cut off, and so were its feet, and it didn't have any feathers. Mommy stuffed stuffin' in its poopy hole, but when it came out, it tasted good!"

The audience loved the unintended double entendre.

Scott took the mike from Beth. "Next we go to our news reporter Mark Goodman, who will give us Goodman family news."

Mark stood up straight, trying to out-adult his sister. "We have big news today. This is the first visit of Grandpa Scott and Grandma Faith to our family. And we wish...Oh, and also Uncle Jon and Aunt Rachel...and Stephie and Jeb. And we wish they'd come again."

Applause.

Stephie provided Oak Park news. "Jeb has another tooth. He had one. And now he's got another. Now he's got two. My mommy and daddy had me, and then they had another. I wish they had another nother. That would make three."

Hilarity reigned.

Scott took the mike back. "And now, radio listeners, we have a musical treat for you, especially those of you who may be celebrating a birthday. Jeb Rockwell will do his rendition of Happy Birthday." Jeb stumbled through his song, aided by the humming of the rest of the family, and Scott closed the premiere broadcast of WARM.

Faith beamed. "Scott, I forget what they call the radio awards, not an Oscar, but you just got my vote."

When Faith had a chance to talk to Rachel alone, she broached a difficult subject. "Rachel, I need your help. You know I'm worried silly about the boys. Jeremy and Jon. And I'm used to being the executive-career-woman-professional who's always in charge. But this thing is out of my hands. I need the family's help."

"Of course, mom, anything."

"Well, I'd like to have a prayer circle today, and don't want to offend you. I asked my priest, you know, Father Whitmore, to see what they did at the ministerial alliance. They have Jews and Muslims, I think Buddhists, too, in their Chicago alliance. So he said if we keep it general, with no 'Jesus' and 'savior' comments, people of different faiths can pray together."

"That's fine. Like I told Jon, my family's Jewish, but I never really practiced the religion."

"Thanks a lot." Faith and Rachel exchanged hugs.

Midafternoon when Jeb went down for a nap and the other three young ones were watching a video, the timing seemed ripe for a meeting. If they waited until evening, Faith and the women agreed, everyone might be too tired. So Faith called the family council to order.

"I know what all of us are thinking about most is Jeremy's condition. We're glad to hear that he's doing well, and we hope he improves. But we need all the help we can get, and I'd like to form a family prayer circle and say a prayer for Jeremy. I'm not as good at this as my newspaper and radio husband is, so bear with me. Let's all stand and hold hands, and put our hearts and souls together in prayer."

Faith paused a few moments as they stood with bowed heads. "Oh God, we come to you as a family asking you for help in time of need. We need your help every day, not just today. But especially today, we pray for your aid and assistance in Jeremy's condition. We ask you to support him and his doctors as they do what they can to heal him. We are weak, you are strong, let us lean on you to enable us to get through this time of trouble. We are unsure of what we should do. Counsel us, we pray, to think and talk and act together. Most of all, we give thanks to you for the love we share as a family, and we pledge to try to strengthen our love for each other as we are strengthened by your love."

They held hands for a moment in silence. Then Melanie and Rachel enveloped Faith in a double bear hug. They were smiling and crying. Jeremy stood motionless, tears streaming down his cheeks. Jon wiped his eyes with his sleeve. After he and Jeremy replaced their wives in the mother-hug, he took out his smart phone and made a notation.

Scott stage-whispered to Faith, "If I'm going to be one-upped by anyone I'm glad it's you. I premiered WARM today, but you inaugurated WHOT!"

They all had a chuckle before they began the serious business of discussing Jeremy's health and the legal hassle to get the medical records. Faith brought them up to date on the latest development:

Doug's demand of a personal meeting for delivery of the medical records. Scott was biting his lip but said nothing.

Jeremy broke the ice. "Mom, you don't want to meet...our father?"

"No, I'd rather not."

Jeremy continued, "He's not too...reliable. You said that before."

Faith nodded and sighed. "That's what our detective's report said. He's doing okay in his business, but he's been married and divorced twice, children by each wife, and another child by someone he lives with. Or did live with. He seems to put himself first, his business next, and family is way down on his list."

"Then why does he want to meet with you?"

"We don't know. My lawyer tried to find out, but his lawyer ended the conversation there."

"What are you going to do?"

"I don't know. That's why I'm asking you people what you think I should do."

Jon jumped in. "Well, mom, I think you have some legitimate concerns. I know you're not just avoiding an unpleasant meeting. You want to protect all of us, right?"

"That's part of it. Our side and his side agreed to a no-liability clause, so that neither of us can make any financial claims on the other."

"And your lawyer approves of that?"

"He says it's about as good a guarantee as we can get."

Jon continued. "Does the lawyer favor the meeting?"

"He knows I don't like it, and he knows Scott is against it. The lawyer says it doesn't make any legal sense, and he's suspicious of it, but he's leaving that up to us. I mean, Scott and me, but I'm putting it to all of you."

Jeremy and Jon were looking at Scott. Jon said to Jeremy, "Are you thinking what I'm thinking?"

Jeremy nodded, and spoke up. "Scott, you haven't said anything yet. You must have some ideas about this. After all, you're the only one of us who has actually met and talked with...our father...recently."

Scott said, "I've been holding back, keeping quiet. Yes, I do have ideas about this. Your mother and I have talked this over. Talked it to death. She's more for the meeting, I'm more against the meeting. Why? Because, excuse me for saying it, but I have met and talked with him, and he's a smooth one. Your mom said unreliable, and keeping the language polite, I'd say untrustworthy. I don't trust him one iota. I don't know why he wants a meeting with her, but I suspect he's up to no good. And Jon has a good point, your mother and I are concerned with protecting the whole family.

"Sure, I may have a biased viewpoint as an outsider, a newcomer to the family, but if you ask for my ideas, there they are. And let me add, my years on the newspaper, interviewing thousands of people, have made me a pretty good judge of character. I apologize if you think I'm badmouthing your father. You can form your own opinions and do what you think is best. Well,...end of story."

Jeremy responded. "Oh, don't worry about our father. He can take care of himself. Thanks for showing us how complicated this one meeting can be."

Scott said, "It can get messy awful fast. If you, your side, agrees to this meeting, he may have up his sleeve meeting the whole family. You know the saying about the camel getting its head under the tent? Well, I'd hate to see this guy work his way into your family. From the first time Faith introduced me to all of you, I realized that she and all of you have a great thing going here. I'm glad you let me be a part of it. And, speaking frankly again, I don't think this guy we're talking about has anything to add to this great group." He hesitated, and everyone waited for him to finish his comment. "To be quite honest with you, he doesn't deserve this family!"

Jon asked, "That's why you don't think mom should meet him?"

"I think it's best for her, and for all of you, if she doesn't. Mind you, I'm not telling her what to do. But if at all possible, I'd weigh in on no meeting."

Jeremy was listening carefully to Jon and Scott. "The doctor said that it would help to have medical records on both sides, but he didn't say it was absolutely essential. So why should we risk family harmony for some medical information that may or may not be helpful to me? Well, to Jon, too."

"And to our kids," Jon added.

Melanie took this as her cue. "Yeah, we'd all like to have the twins' complete medical history if we could, because somewhere down the road, maybe even ten or twenty years later, one of our children might develop a problem, and then we won't be able to get the records. So we want them, but not if it's going to cause pain to mom, and maybe problems for the whole family."

Everyone had voiced their opinion, and although they talked about it for an hour, they couldn't reach any final decision.

Jeremy finally suggested, "I think we should just let Mom handle the situation the best she can, trusting her and Scott to do the right thing."

Rachel added, "Why don't we end with a prayer circle?"

Jeb woke up from his nap, wandering in and insisting on being held by Rachel. The other children took Jeb's whimpering as a signal to rejoin the adults.

Mark asked, "Are you guys playing a game? Can we play?"

Beth piped up, "Is this another radio broadcast?"

Scott joked, "Yes, it is WHOT, live from Springfield."

Faith closed the family council with a simple prayer, thanking God for holding them together and helping them face their problem together.

On the way back to Chicago, Scott and Faith marveled at the unity of this reconstructed family. They knew the hard decision of Tuesday was still on their shoulders, but they felt confident about handling it.

As they drove, Faith took a chance. "Let me try out an idea on you, Scott. You did a great job arranging the detective work on Doug. What do you think about a follow-up?"

"What do you have in mind?"

"Find out what we can about Doug, his relationship with his families, his live-in, and so on."

"You want dirt?"

"Whatever we can get from a private eye. What isn't available as public information."

"As an investigative reporter, I'm all for it. The more we know about Doug, the better we're able to negotiate with him. I didn't want to put it this way to your boys, but know your enemy. I'll set it up tomorrow. How about putting a two-day limit on the snooping?"

"Probably what you can dig up in that time is about all the dirt we need to, or care to, know. You can negotiate the fee, whatever it takes."

CHAPTER 13

$\mathcal{T}$uesday at 9:25 Faith and Scott were in Ludwig's office. They had not made a hard decision, depending on their flexibility and good sense to work out a solution with Bill.

"Come on in, Faith and Scott. Good to see you again. I know this has been hard on you two, but you look upbeat. Do you know something I don't?"

Faith chuckled. "We had a great family gathering with the twins this weekend in Springfield, and still haven't come down from the high of all the shared good feelings."

"That's a good sign. As a lawyer, I can tell you that trials and tribulations test human relationships. Marriages and families either get stronger or fall apart when faced with hard times. If you can hold your kin together in situations as tough as these, your good times are going to be very good."

Faith beamed. "Having their support means a lot to me."

"Uh...how does your family feel about the meeting?"

"They see both sides of the meeting, the up and down sides, and they trust us to make the right decision."

"A unified front! That's what I like to hear."

Scott asked, "Any word from Peoria?"

"Nope. The ball's in our court and they're waiting for our reply. What have you two figured out?"

Scott looked at Faith, put his hand on hers, and waited for her to speak. "Bill, we've been round and round this, and there's no easy answer." She paused. "I don't want to meet Doug, and Scott doesn't want me to. We laid out the options to the family, and they're leaving it up to us. We're not saying that under no circumstances would I be willing to meet with Parnelli. All we're saying now, at this point, is that we'd just as soon not agree to a meeting. Does that make sense?"

"Yes. I'm here to serve your interests. We've already discussed the downside of clients taking matters into their own hands. If you could settle this yourselves, you wouldn't need lawyers, and wouldn't be sitting in these chairs. How do you want me to handle it?" He picked up his pen, ready to take notes on a legal pad.

Scott spoke. "I'm the one who is most against any face-to-face between Doug and Faith. So if we go this route, is there any permanent damage to our negotiating position?"

"Not if I handle it carefully and skillfully. Which I will do my utmost to bring off. In other words, I'll be diplomatic, and not issue an ultimatum that they hand over the medical papers or we'll sue. Those kind of threats are hard to take back."

Faith asked, "What are our chances of getting the records?"

"Hard to tell. Since we don't have any real leverage, I'd say less than fifty percent. Most important, you don't have anything he wants. You have zero to bargain with. And remember, he knows you need the records right away, and he's under no time constraint."

"So you think it's pointless? Useless?"

"No one can answer that except Parnelli. He's the key, the cipher. We'll just have to wait and find out."

"What will you tell Simon?"

"That you see no reason for the meeting. You provided the physician's request for records and we stipulated the non-liability clause. So why doesn't he come up with the papers."

"Is that all?"

"No, that's just for openers. From there I'll try to pry open his door and peek into Parnelli's mind, to find out what's behind the meeting request."

Faith and Scott left the law offices holding hands, less certain about their prospects than when they entered.

Bill Ludwig felt there was no reason to waste time. As soon as Faith and Scott left he placed a call to Simon.

"Hello, Stanley. How's your day going?"

"Can't complain. Busy. You?"

"Staying out of trouble. I just talked to my client about Mr. Parnelli's wish to give her the papers in person."

"She accepted?"

"No. As a matter of fact, she doesn't understand why the papers can't be delivered by U.S. mail, UPS, any service. A personal meeting would mean travel, time, expense. So it seems simpler just to take care of things that way, lawyer to lawyer. After all, we have to earn our money."

"What do you want me to tell my client?"

"Well, of course, I wouldn't presume to tell you how to counsel your client. But if he was my client, I'd say it's eminently reasonable to have lawyers handle these matters. And to conclude negotiations, reach closure, as soon as possible. Release the medical papers and move on."

"Yeah. You and your client might see it that way, but my client sees it differently."

"Can you tell me what he expects to gain out of a personal meeting? For the life of me, I can't understand it. And I can't explain it to my client if I can't comprehend it. So Stanley, I guess I'm turning your question around here. What do you want me to tell my client?"

"As I said before, it's a personal matter."

"These two people have had no contact for three decades, and apparently Mr. Parnelli had no knowledge of...this child...until we notified him. So how could it possibly be personal?"

"I mean personal for my client. Recently he went...back to church...had a religious experience, and he feels a personal obligation to hand over the papers himself. I guess...it's a matter of conscience."

"Stanley, are you telling me the personal reason is a religious reason? And the religious reason is a matter of conscience?"

"That's what my client is telling me, and that's what I'm telling you."

"Well, now, you learn something every day. Stanley, you're a good bit younger than me. I guess that's one of the privileges of us senior citizens, pulling rank with age. Anyway, just let me comment that in more than thirty years of law practice, I've never had a case where a person was willing to go to court, and spend a considerable sum of money, just to exercise his...religious conscience."

"It may seem strange to you, but like I said before, my client doesn't have to hand over these materials. And he doesn't have to justify his motives or procedures."

"Well, there's no way for me to respond to that. Just let Mr. Parnelli know what my client said, and let's hope he's reasonable."

"I'll pass it along."

CHAPTER 14

"*D*oug, I heard from Chicago."

"So when's the meeting?"

"No dice. They see no reason for the meeting, and ask you just to fork over the medical records. Mail them, UPS, whatever, but no personal meeting."

"Is that all?"

"Well, we talked for a while."

"What about?"

"The lawyer and client don't understand why you want a personal meeting, since you haven't had any personal contact for ages. And you didn't even know about the kid."

"What did you tell them?"

"I told them it was personal for you, a religious matter, your conscience."

"Yeah, I guess that covers it."

"Well, the other lawyer, Ludwig, was quite agreeable. I asked him what I should pass on to you, and he said about the same thing as I've been telling you: give them the papers, forget the meeting, close the book on this, you have nothing to gain from the meeting, move on with your life."

"Why would he say that?"

"Because it's true."

"Hah! He's a lawyer." With his free hand Doug held his nose and then waved it as if shooing away an offensive odor.

"Listen, Doug, he and I make money from the billable time we rack up. So it's to our advantage as attorneys to string this out as long as possible, go to court, the whole business."

"You said I might have something to lose. What could I lose?"

"If they file suit, it's not good for you. You've been in court too much for your own good. Pretty soon you'll be on first-name basis with some of the local judges. My best advice to you is to give it up."

"Give it up?"

"Hand over the papers, forget the whole thing. If this goes on, it will get expensive."

"How expensive?"

"You know my hourly rate. And you didn't send the $2500 yet."

"Yeah, I told my secretary to send it to you, but the fuel guy came in and she paid him. I have to keep my trucks and equipment running."

"Well, Doug, green cash is the fuel your legal work runs on, and you've been coasting on empty for a long time. I told you I needed money from you, and you said you would have it last week."

"Sure, sure. I'll get you a check by the end of the week."

"Alright. Just be sure you have the check in this week. Otherwise I can't go forward with this case, because it's going to take a lot of time. For me, time is money. Now back to the Chicago deal. What do you say?"

"I say to hell with this freakin' woman and her uppity Chicago lawyer. They always think they can push around downstate people. Tell them no meeting, no papers!"

"Fine. I'll do that. Against my better judgment. And I can't guarantee where this will go from here. If they file suit, it'll get expensive quick, even if we back out. So come up with some cash, $2500, by the end of the week. And remember, that doesn't pay off your balance, it only brings your account into the range where I'll consider doing more work for you. Bottom line, if you don't fork over the papers, be prepared to fork over some more dough to me."

"How much?"

"Hard to say. Couple of thousand for beginners, could run five-ten thousand if it drags out."

～

"Hello, Bill. Stan Simon here. I was able to contact my client and thought I might as well get back to you right away. I gave him your client's request, and mentioned your general reasoning, but he still wants a meeting."

"Any room for negotiation?"

"You said papers, no meeting. He says no meeting, no papers."

"That's too bad. He's depriving his own child of an important aid to his health."

"Bill, we've been over that ground before. There's still no proof of paternity, and even if we did hand over the papers, we wouldn't be admitting paternity."

"No, the only reason I brought up the angle of the kid's benefit is you said the point of the meeting was...how did you put it? Oh, yes, 'a matter of conscience.' And if we follow that...religious logic...a person who puts conscience ahead of money should put his own flesh and blood's welfare ahead of protracted litigation. But I guess we're not going to get anywhere today. It just seems a shame to me when a matter can be settled. So simply. And permanently. Yet it gets hung up on personal, emotional issues."

"So you're going to take this back to your client?"

"Yes. I have to pass it on. So you tell me. What should I take back to my client?"

"Well, she wants the medical records right away, without any...delay...litigation. If she agrees to the meeting, which my client wants, she can have the records, which she wants."

"Quid pro quo."

"Uh-huh. Papers for meeting."

"Well, I'll be in touch."

~

"Faith, Bill Ludwig. I called Simon, he talked to Parnelli, and the answer is that he still wants a meeting."

"I was afraid of that, even though I was hoping he'd cooperate. Anything more on why he wants a meeting?"

"Simon sang the same song: personal, religious change, conscience."

"What do you think?"

"As a student of human nature, I can tell you that when people become stiff-necked, get their back up, and dig in their heels, they're not likely to give in."

"And that's Parnelli?"

"I can sense his lawyer is giving him the same advice I passed on."

"Which is?"

"Give us the documents, no meeting, move on."

"That's all?"

"Well, if we go to court it's going to cost Parnelli a bundle. Simon had to warn him of that. And I don't think he has a lot of discretionary cash, not with a weak business, and two and a half families to support."

"And he still won't deliver the papers."

"Apparently not."

"So where to from here?"

"The next call is yours. And Scott's. If you agree to a meeting, I'll arrange it. If you want to go to court, I'll start the papers. The first item we'd tangle over is jurisdiction. Canton, Peoria, or Chicago. But we're getting ahead of ourselves. First you and Scott talk it over and tell me what you want to do."

Faith waited until Scott came home to give him the news. As soon as he opened the door she grabbed his hands, and said softly,

"Ludwig says Parnelli won't give us the papers unless he gets his meeting."

"Why not?" He took his coat off and hung it in the hall closet.

They moved to the kitchen and sat opposite each other.

"Same old story. He has personal reasons, because he had this religious conversion, and it has to do with his conscience."

Scott didn't reply, staring down at the table.

"Scott, talk to me. What are you thinking?"

The anger flashed in his eyes. "This is bullshit."

She rolled her eyes. "Well, that's helpful."

"What do you expect me to say?"

"I need your help. And support."

He held his hands out, palms up. "Doin' the best I can, babe."

"I need something better than bullshit."

"Faith, I didn't mean you, I meant Doug. He's full of crap. The question is, how can we shovel it without getting too contaminated."

"Fine. You tell me how we do it."

"By staying as far away from him as possible, having as little contact as possible. I'm just following an Eastern European saying, one handed down in our family: When you touch shit, it just stinks more."

"We agree with that in principle, but what about practice?"

"That's the tough nut we have to crack."

They talked around the issue for more than an hour without making any headway. Finally they decided to give it a rest. Scott suggested they wait until their gumshoe investigator gave them a report, and see if his new information helped them sort things out.

They hired the same private dick as before, because he already knew the territory. His two-day assignment was to ferret out as much as he could about Doug's relationship to his two ex-wives, and the situation of the live-in. And any other dirt. Again, Scott did the hiring and paying, and didn't let Faith know even the name of the agency.

Later that week Scott called Faith early evening, telling her he'd just ordered a pizza and would be home about the time it was delivered. "I've got news from the detective, but it's best to wait until I get home to tell you." He ran into the delivery man as he was getting on the elevator, and brought the square box up himself.

Faith devoured the pizza without tasting it. She was consuming the information Scott relayed between bites.

"Our detective hit pay dirt. And he got lots of dirt. He nosed around, found out from some of the hired help that Doug's hangout is a nearby bar called Shorty's. The gumshoe's best work was seat-of-the-pants sitting on a bar stool swigging beer and shmoozing the regulars. He mined a lot of beer-soaked brains there. So the info comes direct from the source. Not printable in a newspaper, but probably ninety percent dependable. The bottom line is that Doug is an even sorrier cad than we first imagined.

"Not only is he a serial womanizer, but he is a kind of social misfit. Doug is his own worst critic. He's been crying in his beer at Shorty's for some time now, complaining that all the women in his life have done him wrong. His first wife took him for a house and a bundle, and now remarried, lives in the house Parnelli built. From what Doug himself says, even the kids don't have much to do with him, knowing he cheated on the wife and got the secretary pregnant.

"Ditto for the second wife. He built her a new house, maybe to show up the first wife. When that marriage went sour, she copied the act of the first wife, claiming the house and alimony as well as custody of the kid.

"One thing not clear is whether he took up with the live-in before or after the second marriage went on the rocks. But either the guy learned from his altar mistakes, or the woman was too smart to marry him. They had a kid, and she took off with it. If there's any child support, it's a private arrangement, apparently not through the courts."

Faith had eaten her half of the pizza, and Scott had only downed one piece.

"Doug is something else. A womanizer, but definitely not a

family man. And very different from the responsible gentleman described by his lawyer."

"Well, Scott, what—?"

"Wait, you haven't heard the jackpot. The detective was smart, knows how to drop innuendos. He asked, Golly, I can't keep track of all his kids. How many?" And the bartender said no one knows how many, but in addition to the three by marriage and one by live-in, in his younger days he had a paternity suit slapped on him in southern Illinois."

"No!"

"Yes. The detective gave me the location, Pulaski County, and I used my newspaper connections to the courthouse there, and got the basic information. Suit was filed. It came right down to the day of the trial, and it was settled by an out of court lump sum payment."

"So that's the gist of it?"

"Well, there's one more important piece of information that hasn't had time to reach your Horton radar screen. Parnelli Construction is slipping. The company owes a lot of money, and business is bad. So his personal finances must be in very rough shape, what with supporting a handful of families, and his business going down the tubes. The point is he doesn't have the money or the time for a court fight."

"So where does that leave us, Scott?"

"In a much stronger position. If we have to go to court, he doesn't have the money for it."

"It would still take time."

"Yes, courts take their good old sweet time. But you can afford five or ten grand for court expenses. Doug can't."

"Yes. That's the long and short of it. I have plenty of money. He has plenty of time." When she tried to sneak one piece of Scott's half of the pizza, he playfully slapped her hand. She shoved the slice in her mouth, and still chewing it, pranced around the table, throwing her arms around Scott. "You big lug, I lub you."

CHAPTER 15

*F*aith and Scott set up another meeting with Ludwig. They tipped him off through the secretary that they had new information on Doug. Both of them were upbeat when they entered Ludwig's office and laid out the 'dirt' on Doug. Scott made use of his reporting skills to line up the information like a tightly written newspaper article.

Ludwig was impressed, nodding vigorously as he listened. "Scott, let me get this straight. Am I working for you folks, or are you working for me? If you ever get tired of the news business, you can take over our research office."

Scott just smiled.

Faith matched his smile. "Does that put us in a better position? I mean, the paternity case and all."

"Scott, you have the number of the case?"

"It's in the papers I gave you."

"Good."

Faith renewed her question. "Bill, doesn't this give us the advantage?"

"Yes, Faith, I was getting around to that. Two things. First, you're right, the fact that he settled another paternity suit would give us a pattern of behavior to give credibility for DNA testing, and eventual delivery of the medical records. Second, this is the kind of dirt, as you correctly label it, that most reasonable people would not want to come to light, and would rush to settle to see that it was kept buried."

Scott and Faith waited for Bill to continue, but he just stared at them, raising his eyebrows.

Scott repeated, "'Most reasonable people'...."

"That's right, most reasonable people. And I think you two see where this logic leads. Mr. Parnelli seems not to inhabit the domain of rational human beings. If nothing else, his miserable financial condition should tell him to drop this and take care of his business."

Faith frowned. "So this information isn't so helpful, after all."

"Oh, it's useful, alright. But the question still is useful for what purpose. In other words, the decision is still up to you. How do you want me to use this information?"

Faith unclenched her jaw. "What are the options?"

"The option you've exercised so far is still open: namely, to try to keep up the pressure on Parnelli, through his lawyer, to give us the documents. Without a meeting. That's what you prefer, and I support you in this. Unfortunately, Parnelli doesn't listen to reason, and I have to conclude he is not listening to his lawyer, either. I can keep pushing this option, although to be honest with you, I don't see much hope in Parnelli suddenly becoming reasonable. Religious people, it seems, listen to the power of transcendent voices rather than the force of earthly logic."

"The other option?"

"The courts. The courts are eminently reasonable, and here you're absolutely right. The paternity case is the nail in Parnelli's coffin. Simon's posturing about Parnelli being a responsible family man goes down the toilet with that suit. If we had to, we could depose his former live-in. Even if we couldn't get hold of her, the fact that we asked for her to testify would further weaken the argument about Parnelli's character. I can never guarantee the result of a civil case, but I'd say with the paternity suit we improved the fifty-fifty odds to about ninety per cent in our favor. Of course, I'm not happy with that, because I know that for you time is of the essence."

Faith nodded. "Yes. We have the dirt, the evidence. He has the documents, and time, on his side."

Scott asked, "Do you think it's worth pushing Parnelli's buttons?"

"Well, Scott, I never say never. In fact, I would strongly urge you to keep pushing his buttons and never go to trial with this unless every other avenue has been pursued."

"How would you handle it?"

"Lawyer to lawyer. I might as well tell Simon that he'd be a fool to go to court with the evidence we have against Parnelli. And believe me, no attorney likes being made a fool in front of a judge. After all, you never know when you'll come before that court and judge again."

Scott turned to Faith. "What do you think, honey?"

"We might as well try. Sure, what the Hell."

"HELLO, Stanley, how are things in Peoria County?"

"Fine. Not as busy as Cook County, but we make do. Anything new from your client?"

"Well, I was hoping to hear something new from Mr. Parnelli. I've talked with my client, and we think the humane, decent thing for him to do would be to send on the documents. Now I know you and I have talked this over, but we just thought maybe after Mr. Parnelli had turned it around in his head, maybe he'd reconsider. Do the right thing. The charitable deed. As you say, ease his conscience."

"Nope. He's set on a meeting."

"Well, my people don't want a meeting. And taking a thing like this to court, it would rack up a lot of billable hours for you and me, but it would incur a lot of needless expense for our clients. And I know that as his attorney you must have advised Mr. Parnelli how much a lengthy court case could cost."

"Sure! We've discussed that."

"Well, you know it's none of my business...but what we hear about Mr. Parnelli's business is that it's not exactly thriving. Is he prepared to advance the considerable, four to five figure sum that a court case would cost?"

"We've gone over that."

"And he still wants to insist on a meeting."

"Bill, we've already beaten that to death, so what's the point?"

"Well, Stanley, I just think it's a shame he would go to court for a hopeless cause."

"You may think us downstate lawyers can't stand up against a big Chicago firm, but you might be surprised."

"Stanley, Stanley! Did you think I was disparaging your legal skills? Not at all. But if we should go to court, and I bring up the paternity issue— "

"Ludwig, we never admitted paternity, and we're not admitting it now."

"No, no, I mean the paternity case."

"Are you filing papers, then? What good will a paternity suit—?"

"No, not a new suit, the old paternity suit."

Bill Ludwig gave sufficient time for his counterpart to answer, and when he didn't, said, "Well, Stanley, you do know about the old paternity suit, don't you? I mean Parnelli wouldn't stonewall you on that, would he?"

"Look, Ludwig, don't try to bluff me into any admission."

"Why no, of course not. Now if you are unaware of the Parnelli paternity suit, shall I bring you up to date?"

"You can tell me whatever you want to. That's up to you."

"Well, not Fulton County, and not Peoria County. Try Pulaski County. Does that ring a bell?"

"What about it?"

"Oh, I see. He didn't tell you about it. Well, let me do you a favor and mention it now. Always glad to help out a fellow lawyer. I'd hate to bring this up in front of a judge. If you want to look it up, 1982 in Pulaski County, brought up on paternity charges, settled out of court the day of the trial. On the steps of the court house. I can give you the case number if you'd like it."

"No need for that."

"Well, I guess I must have surprised you with that, and you may need some time to talk it over with your client. At any rate, I think you'll agree, with a case like that, any judge would have to look favorably on our client's paternity claim."

"Like I said, I'm admitting to nothing. I'll take it up with my client."

"You do that. And if this helps him to reconsider, that helps all of us. Anything I can do to help your client rethink this, just let me know."

"PARNELLI CONSTRUCTION. Can we help you build a better future?"

"Stan Simon. Let me speak to Doug."

"One moment, please."

"Hi, Stan, how's it going?"

"Not too good, Doug. I just talked to Chicago."

"What's up?"

"A paternity suit."

"Paternity? Hell. They're bluffing. They don't have any witnesses, any proof, and you said I don't have to give any DNA sample. Do those Windy City windbags think they can bluff us downstaters?"

"Doug, I'm not talking about a new paternity suit, an old one."

"Which one?"

"You tell me."

"Uh, I didn't mean there was more than one. And hey, I never got tagged with paternity."

"Well, maybe it never got settled in court. Out of court. For starters, let's begin in Pulaski County, 1982."

"Oh, that one."

"Yeah, that one. Now why don't you tell me about any other ones."

"There was...just that one."

"Thanks for telling me about it."

"You never asked."

"I'm asking now. Any other paternity suits?"

"Huh-uh."

"Any accusations? Some that were threatened but never went to court?"

"That's the only one you need to know about. And that was a long time ago. What's that got to do with the Canton bitch and her medical request?"

"Well, the Canton case...the pregnancy and kid...was also a long time ago. And if we ever went to court, and I try to paint a picture of you as a reliable family man, the other lawyer pulls out this old paternity case, cuts my legs off, and the judge decides against you."

"Well, we don't need to go to court, do we?"

"That's what the other lawyer and I have been trying to tell you. Just settle it. Be done with it."

"Well, if you're working for me, why don't you tell that to the Chicago jerks? Settle it. Meet with me. And be done with it."

"Let's go back to the beginning of your last sentence: if I'm working for you."

"Oh, are we back to that?"

"Yes, we're back to that. And that is $2500, which you've promised me for weeks now. Either you come up with it by Friday, or I have to drop your case and start working for some paying clients."

"Okay, okay, get off my back. I gotta run. Got some customers who may earn me some of your bread."

"Wait a minute! What do you want me to tell the people in Chicago?"

"No meeting, no papers. Talk to you later."

Simon stayed in his office until 5:30, sure that Ludwig's office would be closed, and made his call, waiting for the answering machine to kick in. "Hello, this message is for Bill Ludwig. Thanks for your call earlier today. I talked to Mr. Parnelli, and he hasn't changed his mind. He still says no meeting, no papers. Let me know when you can arrange a meeting."

The next day Bill Ludwig listened to Simon's message and relayed it to Faith. His final remarks to her were: "The ball's in your court. Go to the meeting if you can stomach it. The advantage is speed. If we go to trial, the percentages are in our favor. Never a hundred percent, but ninety or ninety-five percent, thanks to Scott's detective work. The disadvantage is a six- to eighteen-month delay. You talk it over, and let me know."

CHAPTER 16

That evening Faith and Scott sat in their recliners discussing Ludwig's options. Their elation over finding the paternity suit had dissolved into a dismal funk. "Scott, I don't know what to do."

"What do you want to do?" He was staring out the picture window at the lake.

"You know what I want. I want Parnelli to hand over the records. Send them. No meeting. But that's not going to happen."

"No, apparently not. So what's your next best shot?"

"I don't want to meet Doug, would do anything to avoid it, but can't see any way of getting around it."

"Are you dead set on meeting him?"

"No. I'm not dead set on it. But I see myself forced into a corner, with no other choice. What do you think?"

"I think it's a mistake. Well, maybe not a mistake, but a real risk meeting him."

"Okay, spell out the risk."

"First of all, personal risk. It would be upsetting for you. Remember the last time, you only saw him. From a distance. And it threw you for a loop. If you had to meet him. Look him in the eye. Talk to him. Well...I can see it might be much worse."

"Don't you...do you...think I'm strong enough to take it?"

"Sure. Of course you are. But I care for you, and don't want to see you hurt."

"And there's more."

"Sure, like I said at the Springfield family council, this downstate camel would get his big nose into your family tent. And then there's no telling what he might want. Or demand." He spun his right hand in circles by his head. "The guy's gotta be off his rocker. Crazy to be willing to play this out in court."

"Scott, I do appreciate your support. You really are the founding father of our family. If it wasn't for you, I'd still be the lonely old maid pining for her twins, instead of basking in the sunshine of three generations, and sharing life with you. Now I see us at odds on this issue, and I don't want to go against you. Yet I can't help wanting to help Jeremy. I'm torn. Don't know what to do."

"Well, it does seem like you're dead set on meeting Doug. So I don't know what I can say or do to stop you."

"Do you want to stop me?"

"I would if I could. When we first met and you insisted on seeing Doug, I tried to talk you out of it, and then went along with you to try to minimize the damage. Maybe I didn't argue loud and long enough to prevent you from getting hurt. But maybe I'm like my dad. I remember he used to give advice, and then if people didn't take it, he wouldn't push it, he'd just back off and let them do what they had to do." He was still looking out over the lake, frowning.

"So now you're going to back off?"

"I don't know what to do, either. I want to help you, but I can't force Doug to send the papers. Nor can I persuade you not to meet him. There doesn't seem much left for me. To say or do."

Scott got up and slowly walked to the hall closet, getting his coat and hat.

"Where are you going?"

"Out."

"Out where?"

"Out for some fresh air. Don't wait up for me."

"Scott, I need you!"

"I'll be back. Go ahead and try to get some sleep. It'll do you good."

Faith waited a while before she had her cry. But a half hour of sniffles dried up her tears. Then she began to worry. Scott had never walked out on her before. As the hands on the clock reached midnight, she started to resign herself that he might not come home at all. Not that night. Maybe never.

Seldom did Faith want a drink, but this happened to be one of those occasions. She got some wine out of the fridge, then seeing it was almost 12:30, she had second thoughts and microwaved some water for mint tea.

Sitting in her recliner, sipping her tea, she looked out over the lake. She thought, Well, it's just you and me, again. The sky was overcast, and only occasionally did she get a glimpse of the waves.

She rethought her solitary condition. She was not completely alone. She closed her eyes to the world and used Father Whitmore's recommended wireless service to the other world. "Please, God, help me through this difficult time."

After praying, she felt better, but still alone. She went to the bedroom and pulled her journal out of a drawer. Going to her recliner, she opened to a new page.

"Bad times. Terrible times. Trouble. Big trouble.

Scott has been so strong, so supporting.

He's never walked out on me before.

We've never had a big fight.

Maybe there's a side to him I don't know."

She was tired, but didn't want to go to sleep alone.

She set the journal on the side table and went to bed about 1:30 but couldn't nod off. She had gotten used to rolling over in bed and feeling Scott's comforting presence. Now she couldn't stand being alone. The darkness frightened her.

She thought of the retired Cue Bear night light, but cringed at the notion of crawling back into adolescent dependency. Another half hour of tossing and turning forced her to get up, dig the luminous ursine lamp out of her drawer and plug it in. The soft glow of her childhood years soothed her spirits, lulling her to sleep.

Faith woke up as usual at 6:30. Her first order of the day was to get her head straight. She missed Scott desperately. Other mornings she could roll over and snuggle until one of them broke the clinch for a shower. This morning she had to return to her solitary mode.

If she had to handle the Doug situation alone, how would she, how could she, do it? Somehow she'd manage. She always had before. Now she'd have to again. So her mind was made up. Not dead set, but resigned, to go ahead with a meeting. An unwanted meeting with a devil.

Next her thoughts turned to Scott. Where was he? She jumped out of bed, quickly showered and threw some clothes on before heading down in the elevator to the parking level. Her condo unit only had one parking space, but Scott had made a deal with an elderly woman who didn't own a car, renting her space that was close to Faith's. As she suspected, his car was gone. Next she used her cell phone to call her answering machine at work. After a few business calls, there was Scott's message.

"Faith, I just had to get out tonight. I couldn't bear to talk to you about meeting Doug. I need some time and space. I couldn't return tonight. Give me a few days. I love you, babe."

She replayed the message to hear those last four words again. Maybe he wasn't gone for good. But if he wasn't, why did he leave her in the lurch when she had these crucial decisions to make? She went back and forth from the reassurance of "I love you, babe," to the anger of his ditching her.

Whenever Faith felt herself going out of control, which wasn't very often, she sat herself down and carried on a monologue with her inner self. Now she was telling this person inside her: *Calm down. Stay cool. Don't do anything rash. Don't jump to conclusions. Don't do or say anything you'll regret later.*

Knowing she wouldn't be much good at work, she left a message for her assistant Linda. "I'm taking a personal day today, so inform people who need to talk to me, to call me on my cell at home."

She was relaxing over a second cup of tea, watching the sun rise higher over the lake at 8:30 when the phone rang. She spilled some of her tea rushing to the phone, praying it would be Scott.

"Hello, Faith? Father Whitmore. I was surprised to not find you at work, and your secretary said it would be fine if I called you at home. Sick?"

She tried to hide her disappointment. "Oh, Father Whitmore. Hello. No, not sick, just...taking a personal day off."

"Glad to hear that."

"Actually, I'm glad you called. I know we had a meeting later this week, and—"

"Yeah, that's why I'm calling. I'm taking a few personal days myself. Even the preacher has to mend his own fences once in a while."

"Oh....You're taking a few days off later in the week...I was just wondering if today—"

"I'm afraid today's out...I've got a few things to take care of...."

"By any chance would you be coming into the loop? I could meet you if you had time for lunch, maybe."

He gave a short nervous laugh. "No, no loop lunch today."

"Father, I guess it's my turn to be the gadfly. Something's wrong, I can tell. And you don't want to tell me, that's fine."

"A little homework, if you know what I mean."

"You and your wife?"

"Yeah, I've been extra busy, meeting a lot of people, and she's felt shortchanged. So I need to spend some time with her...and...."

"And?"

"And sort some things out."

"Let me guess. The meeting with me in the loop didn't help any?"

"Well, it was one of the straws that strained the camel's back."

"Gee, Father Whitmore, you've helped me out so much. I'm very, very sorry to have added to your problems."

"Don't worry about it. A worse thing for me to fret over would be if I sat in my office alone every week and no one ever wanted to see me. Better to be in demand than in limbo."

"Can I say anything to your wife?"

"No. Please don't. I mean, if you did it would put you inside our marital conversation, and that would make things more difficult. By the way, what did you want to talk to me about?"

"Don't let me add to your troubles. Give me a call when you have time to see me."

"Okay, I've got a deal for you. You pray for me, and I'll pray for you."

"It's a deal, Father."

Talking to him always made her feel better. This time she sensed a mixed blessing. She got a lift in her spirits from just knowing he would pray for her. Yet she knew, at the same time, that she had hurt or alienated the two most important men in her life: first Scott, her soul mate, for going against his wishes, and then Father Whitmore, her soul protector, who had been led astray from his home duties by tending to her troubles.

CHAPTER 17

A little after nine, Faith made the crunch call to Bill Ludwig's office. "Tell Bill to call me at his earliest convenience. He'll know what it's about."

At 9:45 the phone rang and she expected it to be Bill but hoped it was Scott.

Bill's voice disappointed her. "Hi, Faith, called you as soon as I could. Have you and Scott made some kind of decision?"

"Uh, not exactly."

"How can I help you today?"

"I guess you can start the...talking...negotiations...for me to meet with Parnelli."

"Is that what you and Scott have decided?"

"No, not exactly."

"Faith, I'm having a problem in communication here. What is it that you're not telling me?"

"Scott doesn't want me to meet Doug...Parnelli."

"We know that. But he agrees to it, right?"

"No. Not at all."

"And you're asking me to set up a meeting that Scott doesn't agree to."

"That's it."

"I see...."

"Will you contact his lawyer? Simon?"

"Faith, the situation has changed since I last talked to you. You had a united front with your family and Scott supporting you. Now you're going it alone. Is that what I'm hearing?"

"You're hearing it right."

"I can do that. If you're sure you want me to."

"You are representing me, aren't you?"

"Sure. Of course. But the two of you came to see me, and Scott helped out with his detective work. I'd hate to go ahead with this if you and Scott aren't together on it."

"But you will, won't you?"

"Let me see. Tell you what, Faith, I'm kind of busy today, but if you and Scott can come in about 4:15 today, maybe the three of us can look over the options and try to find a meeting of minds that brings all three of us to the same solution together."

"That won't work."

"You're busy?"

"I'm not going to make you dance around this. Last night we tried to talk things over. I was trying to persuade him to go along with me meeting Doug, but he was against it. He walked out and didn't come back."

"Big fight?"

"No. Not a fight. He left me a message at the office saying he needed some time and space. And Bill, I don't expect you to be a marriage counselor. I'm just being honest with you that Scott can't come with me and meet you today."

"Okay, then let's you and me sit down and discuss this."

"Are you against me meeting with Doug, is that what you're saying?"

"You want a straight answer, you got it. Yes. If you had Scott's backing, I'd set it up. But if you and Scott are not together on this, then I think I'd be helping drive a wedge between the two of you. I don't want you to do something you'll regret later. So come by and we'll talk it over. And I'll tell you right now, I don't think we should reach a decision and do something today. I want you to cool down that head of yours and start using your gray matter. Give yourself a few days to let this sink in. There's nothing in this whole matter that has to be settled today."

"Okay, then, I'll see you at 4:15."

Bill Ludwig was valuable. He could have just said "Yes ma'am," and done what she said. And she could have paid the piper. Instead, he thought ahead to the consequences of the actions she asked him to take. And then he advised her to cool down and rethink things.

Yes, she would take it easy. But that didn't mean she'd drop dead. She picked up the phone and dialed Scott's number. When his answering machine kicked in, she hung up and called his city editor.

"Hi, Cal, it's Faith."

"Nice to hear your voice, Faith. But how's Scott? Sick or something? He almost never takes a day off."

Faith had hoped to get hold of Scott, or at least hear where Cal had sent him on assignment. Instinctively, she covered for Scott. "No...he's not sick. Just took a day off."

"Okay, I won't ask what he's doing. He so seldom sicks out on me."

"Uh...you haven't heard from him today, have you?"

"No. Why don't you try him at home? He hasn't shown his face at the paper today."

"Thanks, Cal, I'll try to reach him at home." It wasn't a real lie. Well, maybe an off-white lie.

She was beside herself. Nothing to do. No one to do it with. No place to go. When the phone interrupted her no good thoughts, she prayed: Please, let it be Scott.

Instead, her boss's voice greeted her. The computers went down. Credit card billing and banking services were at a standstill. He begged her, if at all possible, to mount a rescue mission. She told him she'd be there in twenty minutes. She grabbed her cell phone. As soon as she got out of the condo elevator, she called Linda, telling her to order in her usual deli lunch.

By that time she had hailed a taxi and was on her way to the hotel. Then she rang Bill Ludwig, who was able to talk to her.

"Bill, it's Faith. Crisis at the hotel. Can't talk to you now. Can we reschedule for tomorrow?"

"How about the same time?"

"Fine."

Next, she phoned her best computer jockey and asked him for a damage assessment: when and how the system crashed, what data had been lost, what he had done to try to fix the problem. She was still talking on the cell phone to this trouble shooter as she walked across the lobby and went behind the main desk to continue speaking with him face to face. She dialed the hardware vendor on her cell phone, and used a hotel phone to reach the software vendors, keeping both lines open as they slowly worked through the problem, coordinating hardware and software solutions.

It was 2:30 before Faith reached her office. Linda brought in the deli lunch from the office mini-fridge. "Boss lady, you must be starved. I'll hold your calls."

Faith wolfed down the box lunch, checked messages with Linda, and then said, "I'm going to take a horizontal break," her code for a nap. "If Scott calls, or anything urgent comes up, put it through."

She took her shoes off, lay down on her carpet, placed her feet up in a chair, and used a small pillow under her head. She knew she could still make it to Bill Ludwig's office, but after the stress of a computer meltdown, she was too exhausted to think of racing across the loop to his office. In spite of herself, she drifted off.

She dreamed she was in Oak Park. Babysitting Stephie and Jeb. Both of them were crying. They were cold. Faith recalled she had hunted for blankets for Stephie once before, but in her dream couldn't remember where she had found them. The children were crying piteously. Faith was mad, but couldn't quite focus on her anger. Then she remembered. Scott should be helping her, but he had failed to show.

A ringing phone rang down the curtain on the dream. "Hello, Faith Armstrong."

"Hi, Faith. It's Cal. Did you reach Scott at home? I've got a story so hot that he'd kill me if I didn't let him in on it. A city councilman is about to be booted out. I tried to reach him on his cell phone, but he must have it turned off."

"No, I didn't reach him."

"Well, let him know I called."

"Sure."

In her dream she was angry with Scott for not helping her find blankets. Now she was even more mad at him for not making the call that Cal had just placed. She had hoped to awaken to some good news. She had slept a little too long, over an hour. It was just past four. She told Linda, "I'm going home."

Linda said, "You don't look too good. Get some rest."

Usually she approached the condo looking forward to a little down time before she could greet Scott and share the day's news. This day the condo seemed extra dark and empty. She set her cell phone on the side of the tub and drew a hot bath. A half hour soak drained away some of the exhaustion, but nothing would remove the triple worry about Scott, Doug, and Jeremy.

She got out of the tub and dressed. Not knowing what to do, she turned on CNN and tried to watch, but couldn't concentrate, just noticing the news alternate with the commercials. She turned off the electronic eye, going to the refrigerator and taking out some chilled Chablis. She kept the cell phone with her or at her side. Phone in one hand, glass in the other, she installed herself in front of the picture window.

Twilight was fading, and the evening star was granting its first wishes. Looking at the star, she said, "I wish I had a certain someone to share this beautiful evening with."

As dark was settling on the waters, she waited for the moon to throw its beams on the lake and relay them to her. She was ever so thankful she had kept in touch with the lake, even after she met Scott. People come and go. The regularity of the moon, the dependability of the lake, were comforting. And since her cell phone did not speak to her, she used her transcendent wireless to talk to God.

"Please, God, give me the strength to be patient." She prayed through Saint Harriet. "You endured so much in your personal and family difficulties, help me to be as brave as you were." Then she remembered Father Whitmore's advice to pray for. "God, please be with Scott, wherever he is, and bring him back to me."

Prayers concluded, she longed to hear a human voice. She wanted to talk to her family, but dared not. The guys would insist on saying hello to Scott, and she didn't want to make up some lie about him working late. No, she'd just have to tough it out alone.

Dozing in the chair until midnight, she gave up on the possibility of Scott coming home. She picked up her journal from the side table, and stared at the next blank page. She didn't know what to write. Finally she penned:

"Big Trouble!

Help!"

She closed the journal and set it down on the side table. Her scenario of Scott coming home and their having a romantic reunion vanished with the last minutes of the day. Sighing, she headed to bed. A cold and empty bed.

She flicked on the Cue Bear light, ashamed but all too aware she needed its comforting company to make it solo until sunrise.

She got to sleep, but woke with a start, feeling for Scott and not finding him. She got up, walked to her recliner and turned on the light. She had left her journal open. Under her last posting, she wrote:

"Scott, I HATE you!"

She slammed the journal on the side table, then went to bed.

In the middle of the night she woke again, rolled over, and was disappointed again not to find Scott's warmth. Getting out of bed, she went to her recliner and picked up a pen, scratching out "Scott, I HATE you!" replacing it with "Scott I LOVE you!" She felt better when she went back to bed.

The next morning her head reminded her how much wine she had consumed the night before. Two aspirins, a tall glass of orange juice, and a hot bath partially unhung her. Then she had no choice but to go in to the office. The day before she had set up a crash course on how to handle computer crashes. And she'd be working with her head computer honcho to show the mid-level staff how to take care of a crisis like yesterday's if they ever had one when she was away. Usually she turned her cell phone off during training sessions, but today she left it on.

Before noon she returned to her office, and had a message from Cal. "Faith, can you tell me where the hell Scott is? He hasn't returned my calls, and if he doesn't reach me in the next hour or two, his plum story goes to another reporter."

Faith waited until 12:15, sure that Cal would be out to lunch with some of his editor cronies. Then she left a message for him. "Hi, Cal, sorry to be so late returning your call. Scott is out of town. He should be getting in touch with you." She made up what she thought Scott would want her to say.

She managed to make it through the day somehow, leaving just before her appointment with Bill Ludwig.

"HI, FAITH, COME ON IN." Bill looked her over as she was about to sit down, then stood up and motioned her towards him. He gave her a hug. "Honey, that may be the best thing I can do for you today. Let's talk, you and me. If you don't want to, fine. If you do, I'll listen. You and Scott are on the outs?"

"Thanks, Bill, I did need that." She wiped a few tears away and then continued. "Not on the outs. He left night before last, and hasn't come back. Just sent me a message at my office that he needed time and space. Like I told you yesterday. He hasn't even been to the newspaper, and his boss Cal is about ready to kill him."

"Does he drink?"

"No! I mean, he does drink, but he doesn't go on binges, if that's what you're hinting at."

"Not hinting at all, just trying to help you out. If he contacted you, then I'd rule out the maybe he had an accident, check the hospitals routine. First time he's ever done this?"

"Yes."

"Must have been a doozy of a fight."

"Bill, we didn't fight. It was just...a big disagreement."

"To meet or not to meet, that is the question. And the bone of contention between you two."

"Uh-huh. I didn't see any other possibility. He just walked out on me."

"Out?"

"I asked him where he was going, and he said out."

"No threats, no suitcase."

"No. Nothing like that."

"Well, Faith, I knew we were into something heavy when you called yesterday. And let's clear the decks by agreeing that we put off any contact with Simon and Parnelli until Scott shows up and we can regroup."

"What should I do until then?"

"Wait. Hope. Pray."

"Do you think Scott will show up? I mean come back to me."

"I'm sure he will. Yes to both counts. He's a good man, and I'm confident he'll do the right thing. Think of everything he's done for you and your family."

"You're right, all of us in the family say that if it wasn't for him, we wouldn't even be together."

"You don't think he's going to give up on the greatest story he never wrote about, do you?"

Faith managed a smile as he ushered her out of his office, his arm around her.

Leaving the building of the law firm, she decided to walk home. She needed the exercise. Out of habit, she checked her cell phone messages. She had a call from Scott, which must have been blocked by the concrete barriers of Ludwig's law firm offices. "Hi, Faith. No, I didn't fall off the edge of the earth. I'll be home late tonight. I'm at the Trib office now, in the thick of a big story. Cal was ready to fire me. I have to go now. I'll explain everything when I get home. Love ya."

Faith didn't need to walk home. She had cloud nine transportation all the way to her building, and could have flown up to her condo without the elevator.

CHAPTER 18

When Faith reached the condo she knew it would be at least several hours before Scott came home. For him, working late could be eight or nine. To keep herself busy and pass the time, she gave the condo a good cleaning. She started with the refrigerator, clearing out all the crusts of bread, shriveled apples, dehydrated oranges, limp celery, ancient leftovers, antique condiments, and almost-but-not-entirely-used-up dressing bottles. One of the dried up oranges she cut into quarters and threw down the sink disposal to freshen it. She was pleased with the neat look created by the elimination of all those annoying bits and pieces. On the beach they would call these unwelcome objects driftwood, maybe in a refrigerator they should be known as 'driftfood.' She took everything else out and wiped down the walls and cleaned the racks. The final touch was installing a new box of baking soda.

Then she hit the two bathrooms, dumped some cleaner in each stool and returned to the kitchen to wipe down the cabinets, counter, and table. She finished that room using her mop with a new wet paper to give the floor a once over. She went back to the bathrooms, swished the cleaner around in the stools, cleaned the mirrors, and sponged down the lavs. No time for the tub and shower. After all, leave something for the cleaning lady. She wanted to dust, but was running short of time. She pulled the vacuum out of the hall closet and made a quick pass over the carpet. It was seven thirty and she was soaking wet. But satisfied with her thorough cleaning.

She wanted to be showered and fresh in case Scott came home by eight. She was sure they'd make love, and she didn't want to ruin the romantic moment with an intermission for a shower. Actually, physically, she was too exhausted for sex, but emotionally she longed for the intimacy. After her shower she put on her nightgown and a robe, made some chamomile tea, and sat in front of the window. She gazed out at the lake, noticing a few distant glimmers she couldn't make out as ships or reflections of stars.

As she began to doze off, she remembered the night light that had helped her find her way into slumberland the past two nights. She jumped up, hurried into the bedroom and jerked the electrified bear out of its wall plug, apologizing. "Cue, thanks for coming out of retirement to help me out. But your replacement is on the way." She returned to her recliner.

It was past eight thirty. She wished Scott would call! She had blown several hours cleaning, but now she just wanted him home. She leaned back in the easy chair, adjusting the foot rest, and was asleep in a wink.

She awoke to Scott kissing her on the forehead. She tried to get up, but couldn't until she levered the footrest out of the way. In her confusion she spilled her tea on the floor. He started toward the kitchen to get a towel, but she grabbed his arm. "Forget the carpet. Hold me." As she stood up and clung to him, she felt her body shaking.

Scott locked his arms around her. She buried her head in his chest, sobbing as she clung to him. Then with a half-laugh, she stepped back and playfully pummeled him with her fists. "Damn you! Damn you, Scott! I love you so much." And she threw her arms around him again in a bear hug.

"Well, damn you, I love you, too."

They laughed together.

"I want to go to bed with you, Scott, but first I have to hear what you've been doing these two days. I almost went crazy without you. Don't you ever do that again."

"I don't plan to. Don't want to. Well, where to begin?"

"Have you eaten?"

"No. You?"

"No."

"Do you want a beer?"

"Uh, no. Last night, waiting up for you, I had too much wine, so I don't want anything, beer or wine."

Scott laughed. "I'm on the wagon with you, which you'll understand once you hear my story."

"Well, come on into the kitchen and I'll fix us some sandwiches while you tell the tale. And this better be good, or I'm gonna put rat poison in yours."

"Oh, it's good. In fact, you'll find it delicious."

He sat down. "Well, the other night, when I left, I just had to get out, because I saw us headed for a big fight, and I didn't want that to happen. What it boiled down to was you were, or I saw you as, committed to a meeting, and honestly, I was absolutely against it. The immoveable object and the irresistible force. I was sure if I didn't get out, we'd end up saying things we didn't mean, doing things we didn't intend to."

She stopped fixing sandwiches and demanded, "But where did you go?"

"Well, at first, just out, like I said. I walked for a half hour or so, cooled down, and the fresh air helped me think things over. I asked myself, since I couldn't change your mind, what could I do that would make a difference? Well, I figured out something I could do. And there was no point discussing it with you, because you wouldn't agree to it, so I just took off and did it."

"What?"

"Hey, I'm the storyteller, you'll hear it all, so be patient. And hurry up with that sandwich. Ya want a 7-Up?"

"That's about my speed tonight."

"So I came back to the condo, got in my car—"

"I noticed it was gone, and—"

"And I drove to Peoria."

"Peoria!" She dropped the knife she was using to cut the sandwiches.

"Well, I guess I have your full attention."

"Hurry up!"

"Oh, I enjoy this. It was the middle of the night, but I found a sleazy motel in Peoria, and sacked out until about noon. Then I called Parnelli Construction, and made sure Doug would be in that afternoon."

"Oh, Scott." She was watching him eat, but didn't touch her sandwich.

"Next I did my research, buying the Journal-Star newspaper and a Peoria map, and looked over several investment properties advertised in the classifieds. Even called a couple of the realtors who had the listings. By mid-afternoon my homework was complete, so I called and asked Doug if four thirty was too late to discuss some investment properties I wanted to remodel. He said that would be fine.

"I got to his office about twenty to five, carrying the map and the paper with the circled ads. We went into his office and for the next forty-five minutes talked over Peoria real estate, where and what to buy, how much to invest in a property, rental versus resale, remodeling costs. Then—"

"But who did you tell him you were?"

"Meet Rob Anderson, from Springfield."

"No!"

"Yes. I didn't want to give away our Chicago connection. So I gave him a phony address and number in Springfield. Used a street name, Euclid, I saw when we visited Jeremy."

"You devious rascal, you." Faith started to eat her sandwich.

"And Doug does know a lot about construction and real estate. At least in Peoria. I mean, how could he not, being in the business for twenty-five years. By five-thirty I could see he was getting antsy, and I told him I was thirsty, and he suggested we go to a nearby bar. And guess what? It was Shorty's! We each ordered the special, a burger and a beer."

"Scott, what was the point—?"

"You'll learn soon enough."

"I was waiting for him to hit the john so I could grab his empty beer bottle."

"For?"

"For a DNA swab. The waitress grabbed our first beer bottles, and of course we ordered more. Half way through the second I excused myself to go to the car to retrieve my brief case, which I had forgotten to bring in with me. By the time I got back in, he'd emptied that beer and ordered thirds for us. I still didn't know if he'd gone to the restroom. My bladder was about to burst, but I figured if he could hold out, I could, too. After he downed the third beer he went to the john, and I carefully, with a handkerchief, put his beer bottle in my briefcase, so as to preserve fingerprints and hopefully DNA."

"What did you talk about?"

"Let me finish the detectivese first, then the conversationese. We had a fourth, and the waitress picked up those bottles. By the fifth, I was almost under the table, but determined to stick it out and get another bottle. Sure enough, he made a pit stop after he emptied that bottle, and I handkerchiefed it into my brief case. So the double prize of the beer barrel bust is two bottles, hopefully with DNA on them. And fingerprints.

"Talk. Yes, we talked. But once we entered Shorty's, and the beer lubricated Doug, we forgot about construction and remodeling. Doug is a very lonely guy. Estranged from his ex-wives and families. And even from Shirley and their kid. So mostly he was crying in his beer, about never being able to get along with women. Old age is right around the corner for him, and he's worried about growing old alone."

"Scott, his women. Did he mention me?"

"I was getting to that. He was confessing to me, he's done a lot of women wrong, and he can't blame them for hating him. But there's one woman from his past he did wrong, and he just wants to meet her, and she won't agree to it."

"What's the reason for the meeting?"

"He claims he was saved in a religious meeting, and he's trying to do the right thing."

"Do you believe him?"

"Believe what? That he was saved?"

"I mean, that he wants to meet me to do the right thing."

"Well, you're asking me to jump to the bottom line. And I'd sum it up this way. He's a con-man, and I don't use 'con' as a short form of 'construction.' All his life he's been conning others, and right now he seems to be trapped in his own prison, a kind of self-confinement. So now he's conning himself that he's saved and a good guy, for once trying to do the right thing."

"But you don't believe him?"

"I think he believes it, but my pop psychology analysis is that he's shifting from a womanizing egomania to a self-pitying egocentrism. Ludwig told us that his insistence on a meeting is a personal thing, and that person happens to be Doug, not anyone else."

"I think I see where you're going with this, but tell me."

"Yeah, my plan, to return to my intentions in going to Peoria, was to get something that matched Doug's fingerprints and DNA."

"Which you did."

"Keep your fingers crossed. Now if we can just get a lab analysis, we'll have comparison of your and the twins' DNA. And that will be proof of paternity."

"Scott, you're a genius." She gave him a mustard-flavored kiss.

"And if that doesn't persuade Doug to give up the idea of a meeting, nothing will."

Faith put her sandwich down, padded around the table, and sat in his lap. "God bless you, Scott! I love you. Now hurry up and finish that sandwich so we can go to bed and I can show you how much I love you."

"I don't get dessert until I finish my dinner, huh? Well, what did you do while you were waiting for me tonight?"

"Oh, nothing. I just goofed off."

When Scott got home, he had thrown his coat on the recliner, so he went to pick it up and hang it in the hall closet. "Hey, Faith, what's this little pink booklet on the side table? I haven't seen that before."

"Oh, it's just a notebook."

"I thought you kept all your notes on your laptop or your handheld."

"Not everything. Sometimes I like to write things down."

She picked up her journal, and moved into the bedroom. As she removed her robe, she slipped the journal into her drawer.

CHAPTER 19

*S*cott leaned on the same police lab technician who had done the fingerprint analysis of the twins to lift Doug's prints from the two bottles. "Clean prints. Anyone can match this with the perp." The technician couldn't do the DNA analysis, but performed the swab test for saliva samples from the beer bottles, and gave him the contacts for a reliable company used in paternity cases.

Scott contacted the company and agreed to pay extra for a rush analysis comparing Doug's, Faith's, and the twins' samples. The DNA results were conclusive, more than 99% possibility that Doug and Faith were the parents of the twins.

Faith had called Bill Ludwig, letting him know that Scott was back, explaining the reason for his absence. Ludwig's temper flared a little, telling Faith that Scott was playing with fire, contacting a potential defendant in a civil case. Faith reminded Ludwig that, technically, she alone was the plaintiff, and Scott had no biological connection with the twins, so he was actually an outside party. Ludwig conceded the point, at least in theory, but told Faith to try to keep her hubby happy at home, far from Peoria.

When they met with Bill, he was in better humor.

"Scott, I think I know you well enough to tell you this. What you did was risky and foolish. When you hire a lawyer, you don't want to undercut the attorney's work by fooling around with the opponent. But I rush to say also, what you did was smart and very useful. It took a lot of panache to bring off what you did. And so my offer is renewed. When you're tired of the Trib, come head up our research team."

The three had a good laugh.

Ludwig said, "Scott, you picked a good firm for the DNA analysis. These people are reputable. Their results have helped determine the outcome of a lot of cases."

"I had help picking them."

"Good help, I'd say. Well, I suppose the next step is to contact Simon with the blockbuster DNA results, right?"

Faith said, "Yes, and surely he'll hand over the medical records with this evidence, won't he?"

"Faith, my dear, long ago I gave up predicting human behavior. I'm not a magician. Nor a fortune teller. I play the tune I already serenaded you with. Any reasonable person would have given up long ago. And I know you're not thinking of court, but with this substantiating evidence, like the DNA, I can see an almost one hundred percent assurance that a court would side with us."

"No problems?"

"Oh, yes, there would be two problems. First, and foremost would be the time delay, with the other side getting as many extensions as possible. Second, a scuffle over how we got the DNA. But once that's admitted into evidence, the case is a slam dunk."

"Well, go ahead, Bill, and do your thing."

"Yes, I will. I enjoy this kind of work."

"STANLEY, Bill Ludwig. How are you doing? It's been a while since we talked."

"Yes. Uh. Fine. How are you? Well, is your client ready to set up a meeting?"

"I wasn't calling to set up a meeting. I thought I'd just see if your client had had time to rethink, reconsider, and give up on the meeting."

"No. Not at all. Just as determined as ever to have a meeting if your people want the records. He keeps saying, No meeting, no papers."

"I'm sorry to hear that."

"Yeah. So if you don't have anything else, I don't know what there is to talk about."

"The old paternity case didn't even phase Mr. Parnelli?"

"It was a long time ago."

"Yeah. That's the beauty of it. I mean, look at it from my point of view. We're claiming paternity from a 1979-1980 point of time, and the Pulaski paternity case was 1982. Same time frame."

"Well, he doesn't see it that way."

"And he denies paternity?"

"Look, there's no use kicking around paternity for your client and her kid. We don't have to deny it, you have to prove it."

"And what if we did?"

"And how could you do that?"

"The miracle of DNA testing."

"My client refuses to give a sample, and you know you can't force him to, without a compelling reason, which you don't have."

"You know, Stan, I'm trying to help you out here. Suppose I told you that we have a sample of Douglas G. Parnelli's DNA together with his fingerprints?"

"I'd say you were bluffing."

"Was I bluffing when I told you about the Pulaski paternity case?"

"That's different. A matter of public record. Doug's DNA is not."

"Stanley, it's too bad we haven't had an opportunity to play poker. You'd soon find out I don't bluff."

"I don't have time for this."

"Well, humor an old lawyer for a minute. Just hypothetically. If I had Doug's DNA, and matched my client's DNA and her child's DNA, and had a reliable scientific outfit give me a better than 99% match for these two being the parents, would that persuade you to advise your client to hand over the medical records?"

"Cut the hypothetical nonsense."

"Stay with me for just a moment. Hypothetically, would you advise your client to give it up? Or would you like to go to court facing that kind of evidence against you? And have the judge ask you why you didn't settle this out of court?"

"Hell, yes! Hypothetically! But not actually. I've humored you! Now I've got to get back to my day."

"Well, let me add just one thing, Stan. It's not hypothetical. I have all this on my desk. I'm looking at it now. Fingerprints. DNA analyses. And a confirmation from a reputable firm, one specializing in paternity suits in the courts, verifying that the DNA of Doug and my client belong to the parents of her child."

Simon sputtered. "How...how in the Hell...? Well, even if you snatched his DNA, we'd deny it, because you can't prove it's his DNA."

"Good lawyering, Stanley! Don't admit anything. Well, we have a linked set of fingerprints and DNA. Remember a few years back, the federal contract that Parnelli bid on? Unsuccessful, of course. But he had to provide a thumbprint on the application. Public record. We've matched our set of fingerprints and DNA with the fingerprint on the application, so we have his genetic identification, and it matches the DNA of his child."

"Uh...I still don't see how—"

"Well, Stanley, I've tried to help you out, giving away the old paternity case, and now the DNA evidence. But of course you'll understand that I can't reveal the source of my information."

"What...what do you intend to do?"

"Like I said, I want to help you. I want to help Parnelli. First and foremost, I want to help my client. I'm helping you by giving you a preview of what we'd have to offer in evidence in court. I'm helping

Parnelli by making it possible for him to avoid an embarrassing defeat in court. And I'm helping my client by getting her the medical records she and her child need."

"The...evidence....?"

"If you'd like, Stan, as soon as I hang up, I can fax you the summary letter from the firm verifying paternity."

"Yeah, why don't you do that?"

"Glad to be of service."

∾

"HI, DOUG, IT'S STAN."

"Hi, Fiji buddy. How's it goin'?"

"Not so good."

"More Chicago baloney?"

"You might say."

"What do they say?"

"No meeting. Hand over the papers."

"Tell them to go—"

"Wait, there's more."

"What?"

"They have your fingerprints and DNA and have compared your DNA and their client's with her kid's, and it's a match."

"Bullshit!"

"You left me blindsided by the old paternity case, and now this."

"So what?"

"I'll tell you so what. If we went to court and this was thrown in our faces, I'd be the one who was the laughing stock of the legal profession, and the butt of the judges' jokes."

"Well, Stan, after all, I'm paying you to protect my interests."

"No, you're not."

"What?"

"You never paid me the $2500. It's been more than a month since you promised it, and in the meantime all these calls with you and Chicago have added up. I only said I'd take the $2500 because that's what you had at the moment. Right now your account is between $4000 and $5000."

"But we never went to court."

"No, but the time adds up. You spend time building a house, you get paid for it. I spend time building a case, I get paid for it. So either you come up with the $2500, or—"

"Hey, wait a minute, you told me this Chicago lawyer said he had my DNA. Now how the Hell did he get that?"

"You tell me."

"You're the lawyer, so smart ass, you tell me. How do you know he's not bluffing?"

"He sent me the summary from a reliable medical tech firm. And this guy doesn't bluff."

"But for DNA...he'd have to get a sample from me, and I haven't given any."

"Oh, is that right? Who have you been screwing lately?"

"What does that mean?"

"Well, you always bragged that you were never without tail, and since Shirley split, I figured you had someone else to share the sheets. Have you left any used condoms around? You know, DNA can be analyzed from any body part or fluid. That's how rape cases are handled these days."

"You mean, someone could take a rubber I used and check that for a DNA sample? And make it stick in court?"

"Yeah. We could object. But probably the counsel on the other side would ask you to submit a sample to prove that their sample was false."

"Well, what does all this mean?"

"It means, Doug, that it's time for you to give up the papers."

There was no response.

"Doug?"

"Yeah. I'm thinkin' it over. Hell, I've gone this far, why not a little more?"

"You mean you're not willing to hand over the records?"

"Uh...no. If they're so clever to get my DNA, let's see them get the records."

"They'll get them, one way or another."

"Well, I guess it'll have to be another way."

"What is it with you, Doug?"

"I told you, I've changed, and want to show it."

"Well, I'll tell you one thing. I can't represent you in court on this."

"Why not?"

"The judge would throw us out of court and probably reprimand me for cluttering his court with a worthless case."

"Aren't you supposed to be working for me, for my good?"

"Yep. That's what I've been doing. And actually, this Chicago lawyer is doing the same thing. Providing a safe and easy exit to a sorry mess. And you just want to wallow in it."

"Well, maybe you won't stand up for me in court, but they don't know that. So just go back and tell the Chicago mafia that they can shove their DNA papers—"

"I get the point, you don't have to spell it out. But if you don't come up with some money pretty soon, Doug, I'm not even going to make your calls for you."

hen he hung up, Stanley Simon rued the day he had pledged Phi Gamma Delta and become yoked with this frat rat. To save himself further embarrassment, he typed up a letter and faxed it.

Bill,

Thank you for the fax of the DNA letter. Contents of said letter have been forwarded to my client. The position of my client remains unchanged. Mr. Parnelli still insists on a meeting to hand over the medical papers.

I see no point in discussing the matter, so am faxing this to you.

Stanley Simon, J.D.

BILL LUDWIG READ THE FAX, and covered his face with his hands. "GODAMMIT! Goddamn the whole human race!"

"Hello, Faith. Bill Ludwig. Afraid I have bad news. Even the DNA won't dislodge Parnelli from his untenable position. So we're basically back to square one. It boils down to a meeting or a court date. I'm glad you and Scott are back on track together, because now is when you're really going to need each other. Don't rush. Take a few days, and then let me know how you want to proceed."

"That's what I was afraid of. Okay, we'll deal with it."

FAITH WAITED until Scott was home to break the news. "Scott, I appreciate what you did, going to Peoria, doing that detective work and getting Doug's DNA. You did everything you could. And I remember you saying that if this didn't convince him to deliver the records, nothing would. I think that's where we're at. We need to talk."

"Do you want to go out?"

"I'm not even hungry. We've got to settle this."

"Faith, the time for talk is over. It's time to do something. I know the question is not what you want to do, but what you will do. Uh, what you have to do." He walked over to her and gave her a firm bear hug.

After the hug she grabbed his hands, looking into his eyes. "Scott, I only want to do what we agree on together. Without the records, Jeremy's health is clouded. Maybe we can wait a year, maybe we can't. I don't want to take that chance."

"Don't blame you a bit. Okay, you don't want to say it, so let me say it. Your plan is to go ahead with a meeting."

"I see no alternative. And I'd like to hear your support, even if you don't like the idea."

"Faith, you have my support. We've gone through a lot together, so let's get through this. But let's be clear about the plan. And the bottom line is to be as careful as we can meeting this SOB."

"You have some ideas about how to be careful?"

"Right. Couldn't help thinking about it all this time. First, all negotiations to be handled through Bill Ludwig. He'll help protect you and your interests. Second, although I support you, I can't be present. If he saw me, he'd make the connection with Shorty's, and all Hell would break lose. In fact, it would make me a party to the request, and according to Ludwig, it would muddy the waters. It would make the DNA case, if we had to use it, more shaky."

She hugged him, head on his chest. "Scott, you don't know how much this means to me, having your support."

"That's what I'm here for."

"But weak as I am, I'd like to get the family together again."

"Sure, the more the merrier."

A FEW PHONE calls arranged a Sunday reunion at Oak Park.

Jeremy and family arrived Saturday. Sunday morning when Faith and Scott arrived, the kids went bananas. "Grandpa Scott and Grandma Faith are here!"

Mark led the attack. "Grandpa Scott, are we gonna do a newspaper?"

Scott hesitated a split second, sufficient in kid-time for dramatic tension. "Ohhh, noooo, I don't think so."

Groans followed.

Beth led her charge. "Well, then, can we do a radio broadcast?"

Scott put his finger over his lips and looked quizzically at the ceiling. "Ohhh, noooo, I don't think so."

More groans.

The kids frowned.

But Scott met the frowns with an "Ah-hah" wide-eyed look. "I have a better idea."

"A butter idea?" Stephie echoed.

"Yes. Have any of you ever done a television show?"

They looked at each other and all shook their heads in a unanimous negative.

"Well, then why don't we do a television show?"

Mark was skeptical. "How do we do a television show?"

"With a television camera." And he pulled a video camera out of a shoulder bag, pointing it at Mark.

The kids erupted in a victory march through the house. "We're gonna do a television show, we're gonna do a television show."

Scott lined up each one of the kids, and then the adults for a quickie shot of "What I did this last week." Then he took some footage of the kitchen preparation of the meal, and some shots while they ate. After lunch he got comments from the younger set about "What I liked most about lunch." When the dishes were cleared away, everyone gathered in front of the television, where Scott used a lap link to hook it to the video camera.

"And now, ladies and gentlemen, and all the rest of you. We present the premiere performance of the Armstrong Television Family Hour." When he hit the play button, he set off the juvenile pyrotechnics as the kids giggled and laughed at seeing themselves on the boob tube.

Faith didn't eat much. She was happy. Scott had brought this family together. And he had nourished it. She owed so much to him.

Faith's happiness was tempered by sadness. Because she thought of Jeremy's condition, and the family council she had asked for. After the family TV program, Rachel shooed the kids into Stephie's room for a video.

The family prayer circle had become a tradition. Everyone joined hands as Faith gave her prayer. "Our father in Heaven, we come in thanks today for this lovely family. We are grateful to be able to share food and love with one another. We owe our happiness to you. We also come seeking your help in this time of trouble. We ask you to take care of this family, and to help us through sickness. As we face difficulties, we pray that you will be with us and help us to make the right decisions, do the right things. Amen."

Rachel surprised Faith by asking, "Can I add a prayer?"

Faith murmured, "Of course."

"God almighty, Lord of Heaven and earth. We are weak. You are strong. Watch over us, we pray, as we watch over each other. In health and in sickness, be with us. Help us. Guide us. Lead us. Most important of all, be with us as we walk together through these difficult times. Amen."

Faith gave Rachel an extra-long hug.

Then Faith, with Scott's help, laid out the latest development brought about by Scott's escapade in Canton and Doug's stubborn refusal to give up the documents. Gingerly, Faith paved the way to the plan, supported by Scott, to go ahead with a meeting, taking care to control the situation. Several times Jon and Jeremy tried to ask questions, but Rachel and Melanie trumped their spouses each time, Melanie saying "We've heard enough," Rachel adding, "Don't put her through this again, guys."

Melanie announced the consensus of the council: "Mom and Scott did okay up to this point, so let's just leave it up to them to do what they think is best." The twins realized that once this decision was reached, there was no point in pushing any of the particulars.

PART III
MEETING THE DEVIL

CHAPTER 21

On the way home, Faith asked, "Scott, where do you come up with these ideas? I mean, a television show."

"Blame it on the kids. They bring out my creative side."

"And Rachel! That was a big surprise."

"Big surprises come in small packages. She's a sleeper. Much stronger than you'd ever suspect."

"She was tremendous today. Helped me get through the meeting. And in some ways, the wives were the unifying force. The guys were kind of tentative, dancing around the issue. The gals just picked it up and ran with it."

"You've got two great daughters-in-law. Your twins know how to pick 'em."

"Well, Scott, now we've got to talk about the biggie, the meeting."

"Yeah. Let's set up a parlay with Ludwig, and he'll know what to do. I trust him, but I'd still like to be there when the plans are made."

LUDWIG MET THEM WITH A SMILE. "Faith. And Scott. Good to see you again. And we've met so many times, and thrashed this around so thoroughly, all I have to ask is do you both agree to a meeting with Parnelli?"

Scott and Faith nodded. Scott said, "We don't like it, but to speed things along, we'll agree to it. And we depend on you to set it up with safety and assurances."

"You're absolutely right. Ground rules. Since he wants the meeting, we set the place. In my offices."

"Good," Scott said.

"In my offices, with me present, and his attorney. I can shield Faith, he can muzzle his client if necessary."

"What else?" Faith asked.

"Agreement ahead of time, as to the duration of the meeting, let's say thirty minutes, and at the end of that time he hands over the family medical records."

Scott looked at Faith. "Sounds good to me."

She asked, "What do we do for a half hour?"

"Well, Parnelli can talk it away if he wants. He can ask what he wants, too, but the only thing we agree to do is to meet him. We don't give him any information. No names, addresses, phone numbers. In fact, we'll both be careful only to mention 'the child,' not even using gender-specific he/she or his/her."

Faith added, "And of course not letting on there are twins."

Ludwig nodded. "Well, Faith, I can see why you're a veep, you're a thoughtful negotiator."

They agreed to let Ludwig set up the meeting, giving him some available times for them.

∽

"HELLO, Stanley, Bill Ludwig here. How are things going?"

"About the same. You got my fax?"

"Yes."

"Well, like I put it in the fax, unless you have a deal for the meeting, we're wasting each other's time talking about it."

"That's what I was calling about."

"A meeting?"

"Maybe. My client is quite magnanimous. We are confident a court would rule in our favor, but our primary concern here has been the speedy resolution of the matter of the medical records to help safeguard the health of her child. If Parnelli can agree to a brief meeting and assure us he will hand over the medical records at the conclusion of that meeting, we are willing to discuss it."

"Shoot. What do you have in mind?"

"Brief. Thirty minutes tops. And since he wants the meeting, which means we're meeting him more than half way, the place is my firm's offices here in Chicago. You representing your client, I representing mine. Four people. That's the offer."

Why don't you fax me the details, and I'll show it to my client."

"Remember, Stanley, time is of the essence. We'll make this offer good for one week. The meeting to take place the following week. After that, we still have the option of going to court. And I don't think you want to drive this shaky case into court."

"I always want to avoid court."

"DOUG. STAN."

"Uh...Stan, I'm kind of busy. Can you call me back?"

"No, I can't. I need to talk to you. Now. About a meeting."

"Great. They came across, huh? See, I told you we could do it without going to court."

"Here's the terms, good for one week: thirty-minute meeting in the lawyer's Chicago offices, you and me with her and her lawyer. They meet with us, and at the end of the thirty minutes we hand over the medical records. Is that a deal?"

"Why do we have to go to Chicago?"

"Because, stupid ass, you asked for a meeting, and they're accepting your demand, so they set the time and place. Didja expect them to come down and have a beer with us at Shorty's? You know this isn't a frat reunion."

"Don't get hot and bothered. I'm thinking about it."

"What's to think about?"

"We don't have to accept all the conditions, do we?"

"It's like real estate, offer and counter-offer. Is there something you don't like about it?"

"Yeah. The law offices. I got a bad taste in my mouth from all the shit we've had to eat coming from that office. So make it a different place. You know, neutral territory. And how about an hour?"

"Christ, Doug, what do you want an hour for? You haven't seen this woman for more than thirty years, so what do you want to talk about? Certainly not the latest sports scores."

"Well, try for those conditions. Gotta go. By."

Stanley relayed these two conditions to Bill Ludwig, and Bill relayed them to Faith and Scott. They asked Bill's advice.

"The important thing is they agreed to come to Chicago. I'd prefer my law offices, but realize that may be overwhelming for these downstate rubes. I know a restaurant where we could go. In fact, I have a certain table I use for such purposes, by the kitchen, not next to any other tables or booths. The kitchen noise helps cover your conversation, and no one else is close enough to over-hear. More important is sticking to the half hour maximum. That will cover the basics. After that it can get tedious and hairy. We put up with a half hour of his monologue, sip our coffee and water, and then we get the documents."

They agreed to these amendments of the conditions, and Ludwig relayed them to Simon: a thirty-minute meeting in a steak house, with the papers handed over at the end of the half hour. Ludwig confirmed available times and had his secretary fax directions to the restaurant.

"Doug. Stan again. Okay I think we have a deal. They agree to meet in a loop eating place, but stick to the thirty-minute max. Can you agree to that?"

"I guess so. Half an hour is better than no hour at all, huh?"

Simon didn't laugh. "Okay, they've given us a window of three days next week, Tuesday, Wednesday, or Thursday at 2:00. They gave us the directions to the restaurant, and we'll ask for Mr. Ludwig's table."

"I'm busy with a big remodeling project all next week."

"Hey, Doug-meat, you wanted a meeting, they give you one. Pick one of the three days. We can drive up mid-morning, catch an early lunch, and be at the restaurant by a quarter to two."

"Yeah. Okay. Thursday. That way I can make some headway on my project. Now I gotta get back to some customers."

"Just a minute, Doug! You didn't get me the $2500, and now your account is over $5000. The trip to Chicago will be a full day, maybe ten hours of billing. So I see $3500 by Monday, or I don't go to Chicago."

"Cut me some slack, pal, will ya?"

"You've had all the slack I could afford. And don't give me any postdated check, or say you'll give me the cash when you see me next Thursday."

"Sure, Fiji buddy, I hear ya. I'll get you your dough.

Simon passed on the acceptance to Ludwig, who relayed it to Faith and Scott.

CHAPTER 22

The following Monday, Simon still had not received any money from Doug. Just before five he called Parnelli Construction, and was told Doug was out in the field. He called Doug's cell phone and got an answering service. On a hunch, he called Shorty's, and the bartender said he was lucky, Doug just walked in.

"Oh, hi, Stan, major problems today. Cement truck broke down just as we were trying to pour a foundation. Couldn't get back to the office all day. Was going to get that check to you."

"Well, Doug, don't bother. You've been promising me money for months, and I've got to move on. I won't be able to represent you. Not until you pay your account in full. I'll have my secretary mail out an up to date bill."

"Stan, don't poop out on me now. Hey, we've got a meeting this Thursday."

"I don't."

"What am I going to do about it?"

"That's for you to figure out." He hung up, and didn't answer the phone, typing out a letter to Ludwig.

I regret to inform you that as of today I no longer represent Mr.

Douglas G. Parnelli. Should you need to contact him, you can reach him at Parnelli Construction Company.

Simon faxed the letter to Ludwig.

Tuesday morning Bill Ludwig snatched the lone fax out of his machine, and swore to himself. Before contacting his client, he had to learn what he could from Simon.

"Hello, Stanley. Just got your note. Quite a surprise. Anything you can tell me?"

"No. The letter says it all. I no longer represent Mr. Parnelli."

"Well, you know I've tried to help you out in the past, giving you information I didn't need to. Maybe you could help me with two non-controversial pieces of information. One, is the meeting still on, and two, does Parnelli have other representation?"

"Yeah, Bill, those are non-controversial, and I'd be glad to help you, but I just don't know. The best I can suggest is you contact Parnelli and ask him."

"Any hints about how you happened to part company?"

"You know that's privileged."

"Yeah, I just thought you could share something with me. Off the record, of course. Actually, I sympathize with you. Having a client as impossible as him must have been trying. And you certainly couldn't take his case to court. The judge'd throw you out on your ear. We know he and his company are both pretty shaky financially."

"I can't comment on that."

"Yes. I understand. Pardon an old man for just thinking out loud. Well, if anything changes, I mean, if you are representing him again, let me know."

"FAITH, Bill Ludwig here. Strange development. Got a fax this morning, sent late yesterday, that Parnelli's lawyer, Simon, is no longer representing him. Tried to squeeze Simon for some information, but he's tighter than a drum, won't give me any clues. I'd have to guess since they've come this far, it's a money problem."

"My God. What should we do?"

"In other cases, I'd keep hands off until Parnelli secures another lawyer. But a new lawyer might require a retainer up front, and finances may be the very reason why Simon dropped him. Well, I take that back. Parnelli could have dropped Simon, but I would expect the former."

"'In other cases'...but in this case?"

"Well, we've worked long and hard to set up a meeting. If you want the records PDQ, then we could go ahead with the meeting, minus Simon."

"How would you arrange that?"

"I'd have to contact Parnelli directly. Don't like to do it. In fact, the first thing I'd have to ask him is if he has legal representation, and if he wants me to talk to his lawyer. That's the protocol. He may have snagged another lawyer. If he has, the new guy will want some time to go over the papers."

"Let me call Scott and see what he says."

She let Scott in on the bad news. His advice was to move ahead. The worst part of the whole affair was the waiting and anticipation. She called Ludwig back and asked him to contact Parnelli.

"Hello, this is Bill Ludwig of the law firm of Ludwig, Franklin, and White. Could I speak to Mr. Parnelli?"

"One moment please."

"Yes, Parnelli here. How can I help you?"

"Mr. Parnelli, this is Bill Ludwig. I've been in discussions with your attorney, Stanley Simon, on behalf of my client. Yesterday Mr. Simon sent me a fax stating that he no longer represents you. I confirmed that with him by phone this morning, and he's the one who gave me your phone number. Let me ask you first if you have obtained other legal representation, because if you have, and wish me to contact your lawyer, then that's the next thing I'll do."

"Stan...Simon already contacted you?"

"Yes. Sent me a fax yesterday, and I checked with him a few minutes ago. I asked him if you had someone else representing your interests, and he said I'd have to ask you, because he didn't know."

"No. No, I don't. Does that mean the meeting is off?"

"Well, it does change at least one condition. I will be representing my client. And Simon was going to represent you."

"And if he doesn't?"

"Well, you're entitled to get any lawyer you wish."

"And if I don't?"

"That's up to you...I guess you don't need representation. It's up to you to exercise the option of representation by Simon, someone else, or come without formal representation."

"Yeah. That's what I'll do. I don't need a hotshot lawyer representing me."

"You do have the medical records?"

"Yeah. Sure."

"And you will bring them with you to the restaurant?"

"Yeah. Sure."

"Well, Mr. Parnelli, usually these details are handled by lawyers, and I hate to bother you with them, but Mr. Simon, when he was representing you, did forward to our office your signed agreement to the effect that at the end of the thirty-minute meeting you'd hand over the records."

"Sure, I said I would, and I will."

"Yes, I'm sure you will. You understand I'm just representing my client, and reminding you that even though Mr. Simon no longer represents you, the document you signed and he forwarded to me is still a binding agreement."

"Yeah. Of course."

"Well, I have a map and directions to the restaurant, so give me your fax number and I'll have my secretary send them directly to you."

"Faith, Bill Ludwig. We're still on with the meeting. I talked with Parnelli. He doesn't have another lawyer, which makes me sure that Simon dumped him. If Parnelli had done the firing, he would have hustled up another lawyer. Simon probably pulled the plug on him for lack of payment."

"Bill, what difference does it make if Simon isn't there?"

"There's an advantage to us, because it means I don't have a legal jockey opposing me. The disadvantage is that if Parnelli gets out of line, tries to fudge on the agreement, or overstep the bounds, time-wise, and so on, Simon is not there to hold him to it."

"Some risk."

"Right. Some risk."

"Acceptable risk?"

"We're back to the tradeoff. We've come a long way to reach the delivery of the records, and if we want speedy delivery, the only way to go is forward. If we wait for Parnelli to secure legal counsel, we're talking at least another month, maybe two."

She called Scott, who agreed with Ludwig, there was no point backing out now.

Bill phoned Parnelli's office. The secretary confirmed that the directions to the restaurant had arrived, and that Mr. Parnelli had arranged to be in Chicago Thursday. Ludwig figured the less pre-talk with Parnelli, the better, so he didn't ask to speak with him.

CHAPTER 23

ednesday night, Faith was nervous. Several times she came to Scott and had him hold her. He smiled at her. "You're tough, gal. I didn't want you to have to go through this, and did all I could to prevent it. But you'll make it."

She went to bed with him, too anxious to make love, but snuggled as close as she could. After he started snoring softly, she got up quietly, tip-toeing in to the picture window. The moon was not visible, behind her building. Fluffy clouds scudded above the lake, lightly illuminated by the hidden moon. The lake was inky blue-black, unfathomable. She had Scott's support. She cherished her family's encouragement. And valued Bill's advice. Yet she needed the comforting presence of the lake. And she silently asked the powers above to be with her.

The next day, Faith decided she might as well go to work, rather than sit around the condo and fret all morning. Bill Ludwig wisely suggested that the two of them have lunch at twelve-thirty, and they could linger over coffee, waiting for Parnelli to show. She knew that he was being nice, helping her relax. What a thoughtful attorney!

About half past eleven Faith got an emergency call from the front desk. The computer system was acting up, and it looked like it might crash. She grabbed her cell phone, called Bill Ludwig, and said she'd have to handle this emergency. She suggested they meet at a quarter to two. Bill corrected that to one-thirty. She agreed, and had Linda order in a lunch for her.

Why was it, she thought, whenever she had a meeting with Ludwig, the computers misbehaved? Fortunately, it was a simple glitch, and it only took a half hour to correct the problem and give the office people a refresher on how to handle these problems. She had time to go back to her office and at least nibble on her lunch. She couldn't face the meeting on an empty stomach.

By one-fifteen she was out the door and at the restaurant just before one-thirty. She asked for Ludwig's table and saw how perfectly it was situated, nestled just outside the kitchen, away from any other tables. She wasn't familiar with the restaurant, a moderately priced and modestly decorated setting that was too downscale for any bigtime lawyers like Ludwig to consider for entertaining clients. That would make it much more discreet, a location for confidential talk away from the favorite lunch places for loop attorneys.

But Ludwig wasn't there. She whipped out her cell phone and called his office. The phone rang interminably until an answering machine kicked in. Swearing, she dialed again. Repeat performance. She told herself not to panic. Maybe they had phone problems. At one-forty-five she got a breathless answer, "Ludwig, Franklin, and White Law Offices."

"I'm calling for Bill Ludwig."

"Well, all I can tell you is he's doing fine, everything considered."

"What do you mean?"

"You know he had an attack?"

"An attack?"

"A heart attack."

"When?"

"I don't know. It's been chaos here. Not too long ago. In his office. The paramedics took him away in an ambulance, and we heard he made it to Michael Reese Hospital. That's all we know. I have to get off the line. The switchboard's going crazy."

Faith looked at her watch. Ten to two. No time to call Scott, and after all, what could he do? He couldn't rescue her, and couldn't even risk being seen nearby. Faith made a quick decision. She'd have to fly solo. She had to meet the devil Doug alone. She tried to remember Scott's advice: be careful. And if you touch shit, it just stinks more. She'd be on her toes, not giving away any information. And she'd keep her distance from him, both physically and emotionally.

Bill's medical condition helped her put things in perspective. She wasn't battling for her life, she was just undergoing some temporary unpleasantry. She had taken the side of the booth backing up to the kitchen, so she could spot people entering the restaurant. A waitress made her second trip to the booth, so she ordered an iced tea. Something to keep her hands occupied.

The hands of her watch slowly crept to two. No one showed. She was debating with herself how long she should wait before walking out.

Five past two. Ten past. She decided a quarter past was her limit. She'd leave a nice tip for the waitress's trouble, and go. Doug rushed in just before she was about to leave.

The hostess brought him back to her table. Strange, she thought, she wasn't that nervous.

As the waitress left, he ordered a cup of coffee.

He slid into the booth, a little on edge, and extended his right hand, but she kept hers wrapped around her iced tea, and he quickly withdrew his. In his left hand he was clutching a thin leather brief case. "I...appreciate you meeting me...I'm Doug, and you're...."

"Faith."

"Yes, Faith. I thought—"

She said calmly, "Mr. Ludwig planned to meet with us, but won't be able to make it."

Doug managed a smile. "Good. We don't need lawyers to talk."

"You brought the papers?"

"Yes." He patted the brief case.

"Could I see them?"

"They're there. Family records. Medical records."

Faith pulled a travel clock out of her purse and set it by the wall so that both could see it. "The agreement was for thirty minutes. It's now two-fifteen. At two forty-five you hand over the records."

"Sure. Sure. I keep my word."

Faith was keeping his words, too. When she retrieved the clock from the purse, she turned on a mini recorder in her purse, and set it at the side of the table, so it would capture both of their voices.

Doug was nervous, facing this mature woman in a power suit. He had come very casual, slacks and a golf shirt with an open neck. "Well, I guess the first thing I should do is apologize for putting you through all this trouble."

He waited for her to accept the apology, but she sipped her tea. Long ago she learned as a Horton executive to assume an expressionless facade, neither happy nor sad, not angry, not conciliatory. Betty Foutch had told her to practice this "poker face" in front of a mirror. Faith nicknamed it her "hotel face."

Doug filled the awkward silence. "I mean, sure, I could have just sent the records on, but I wanted to meet with you. I've done some wild, crazy things in my day, and I sure did bad with you. Of course, I never did know that you had a baby. That would have made things different. So I did want to say I'm sorry for...that. I mean, getting you pregnant."

Faith was silent, gripping her glass of iced tea, staring at him.

Doug gestured with his hands to try to reinforce his rambling talk. "I should have known better. I was in college, and you were just in high school. And you were so pretty, I couldn't resist you."

Faith's face reddened, but she maintained her neutral expression.

"Well, that's the way I remember you, but you're so different now. Well, still pretty. But a grown woman. Of course, I'm a little older, too." He tried to get a laugh but failed.

"Well, the reason I went to all this trouble...to arrange this meeting...was to apologize, ask you to forgive me."

A slight wrinkle appeared on her forehead. "For what?"

"For getting you pregnant."

"I never blamed you."

"You didn't?"

"No. It was my mistake."

"It was my mistake, too."

She shrugged. "If you say so." She pursed her lips tightly.

"Well, I...don't know what to say...now that we're here. Maybe you have something to say...or ask."

She asked, slowly and deliberately, "Yes, what was the purpose of this meeting?"

"I told you. To ask you in person to forgive me."

"You've done that. So if the purpose of the meeting is taken care of, why don't we end it here?"

He bristled. "Not so quick. We've still got some time on the meter. Do you forgive me?"

She gazed at the ceiling, as if requesting heavenly assistance. "If you want forgiveness, you have my forgiveness."

"Doesn't sound like it."

She retorted, "You asked for it, you got it."

"I guess what's weird about all this is that you and your lawyer know everything about me, but I don't know anything about you. I guess things must have been difficult for you...pregnant in high school."

"Yes. Very difficult."

"And how did you manage...?"

"I managed."

"I mean, did you get married, and have...other kids?"

"I'd rather not talk about that."

"You know I have kids."

"Yes."

"Three. Two by my first wife. One by my second." He paused and looked at her. Although she was expressionless, he added, "And I guess you heard I had another with my live-in."

"Yes."

"You know everything, don't you?"

"I know about the paternity case."

"You can see I've been a heel, a no-good, all my life. And you probably know my two families have turned against me, and my live-in moved away with my kid."

"So I understand."

"When I heard about you, after all the dumb and dirty things I've done, I wanted to do it right, come to you personally, and apologize."

"Yes. You've done that."

"Well, yeah, but it's not that simple. I've sure messed up my life. And I can tell by the way you dress, you've done alright."

"I got by."

"I bet. Me? I'm practically alone in the world. My business, that's all I've got, and business in Peoria is tough any time. Real rough now."

"Times are difficult."

"You know what I did? Some of the guys in my construction crew, they're as hardcore as they come, but a few of them got religion, and when I was whining and complaining to them, they talked me into going to church with them. And I accepted Jesus, got saved, and now I'm trying to be a better man. A better person. And that's the real reason I wanted to see you, in person, to give you these records. Do you understand?"

"No, not at all. My child has been in desperate need of these medical records. And you wouldn't give them to me without a meeting. This has delayed the diagnosis and treatment of my child's condition. The only reason I agreed to meet with you is out of concern for my child. Do you understand that?" The longer she spoke the more passion she inflected in her words.

"I can't blame you for hating me. For getting you pregnant long ago, and for holding up the records. Maybe that was selfish of me, but I had to do it for my own sake." His eyes were fixed on his coffee cup.

"Yes. What you did was for your sake. What I'm doing, agreeing to this meeting, is for my child's sake." She continued to stare directly at him.

"Well, yes, you're right. I've been a selfish jerk all my life, and for once I try to do something right, and it still comes out selfish."

Faith didn't comment.

She let him thrash in his self-pity until his half hour was up and then she reminded him, "The half hour is up. Give me the records."

He slowly pulled them out of the brief case and passed them to her.

As she quickly scanned them, surprise and then anger spread across her face. "I see your records. And your parents'. But what about their siblings' records?"

"Uh...they're dead, and I couldn't get them," he mumbled.

Faith's voice was shrill. "Mr. Parnelli, the agreement was you'd provide your own, your parents' and their siblings' records."

"Well, I couldn't get them." He tried to laugh it off.

"Why not?"

"Most of them are dead, and some are scattered. I do run a business, and it was hard enough getting my folks' stuff."

"My lawyer is not here, but you will hear from him. We had an agreement, and you haven't kept it." She glared at him.

"Well, too bad. I gave you what I could get."

"Our meeting is over."

"Just a minute. You didn't give me your name."

"No, I didn't."

"And you didn't even tell me if my...child...is a boy or girl."

"No, I didn't."

"And you won't?"

"No, I won't."

"Now wait a minute. I came all this way to Chicago, and you won't even talk to me for a few minutes? I'd like to meet with this child of mine. You can't blame me for wanting to see my own kid."

"Coming to Chicago was your choice. Having a meeting was your idea. I've met my part of the agreement, and you haven't. Now if you're not going to leave, I am."

"I'm not leaving until you tell me about this kid...son or daughter...."

She shook her head, and then as she started to slide out of the booth, he quickly stood up and blocked her exit.

Quietly and firmly she said, "Mr. Parnelli, if you don't move, I'll call the manager and tell him you are harassing me and ask him to escort you out of the restaurant."

"How can I contact you? Or my kid?"

"Any contact with me will be through my lawyer."

He moved aside with a sneer on his face.

She walked out of the restaurant without looking back, and hailed a cab. In the safety of the taxi, she thought to herself: I met the devil. Alone. And didn't let him drag me into his personal Hell.

CHAPTER 24

*I*n the taxi she called Scott, asking if she could meet him at the Trib offices. Listening to her voice, he told her to come right over.

His desk, in the midst of a sea of cluttered desks, was not the ideal hug-site, but she needed Scott to hold her. He put his arms around her.

They talked as they walked to a nearby coffee shop.

"You okay?"

"Yeah, but Bill Ludwig isn't. Heart attack."

"During your meeting?"

"Just before."

He stopped in mid-stride and turned her to him. "You mean you met that asshole alone?"

"Yes. It all happened too quick. I followed Bill's and your advice. Be careful. Go forward, not back."

"Was it worth it?"

"Yes and no. He handed over his own and his parents' records, but not their siblings'."

"Why not?"

"Too busy. Too lazy. Too dishonest."

"The bastard."

"A real SOB."

"How did you handle it?"

"I taped the whole thing, so later you can play it back."

"How did it go?"

"Actually, I surprised myself and stayed cool. I was already at the restaurant, a few minutes before the meeting. I had a mid-morning crisis and had to skip lunch, and then when I got to the meeting place, Bill wasn't there. I called his office and found out he had a heart attack. That was ten to two. I either had to jump ship or go ahead with the meeting."

"You didn't tell Parnelli?"

"No, just that Bill couldn't make it. And pretty much, you'll hear it, I let him do the talking, and just responded. And didn't give him any information at all."

"Good girl."

He was holding her hands. He drew them to his lips and kissed them. "You're a heck of a lady. I sure know how to pick 'em."

She drew his hands back and kissed them. "You're a heck of a man. Gentleman. I sure know how to pick 'em."

A FEW DAYS later Scott and Faith went to see Bill in the hospital. The head nurse told them they could only stay a few minutes. Entering Bill's room, Faith was shocked. Relieved of his three-piece suit, deprived of his massive desk, removed from his large corner office, Bill was reduced to a pathetic pale blue gowned occupant of room 1247. A tangle of electrical cords ran from his chest to a heart monitor, an IV drip was hooked to his wrist. Powerful attorney Bill Ludwig had been reduced to a numbered but power-less patient.

He looked up, his ashen cheeks forming a weak smile. He cleared his throat and croaked a hoarse "Hi, you two." All that he retained of his former commanding authority was his voice, driven down to a raspy bass by the irritation of oxygen tubes during his surgery.

The nurse came in and laid down the law. "Five minutes. That's all. And don't upset him"

Bill roared "Bullshit! We'll talk as long as we want."

The nurse slowly walked over to the bed, patted his hand, and spoke gently but with authority, "Now we're talking nonsense again. And we can't have that, can we?"

Bill turned his head away.

The nurse held his hand, and cooed, "What's it gonna be? Do you want your five minutes?"

"Okay, you win."

"Now that's a good boy."

The head nurse glanced between Bill and his well-wishers. "We're watching the monitor at the nurses' station, and if there's any change, you're outa here."

Faith hadn't seen a synthetic smile like that since the days she spent at the Canton adoption agency with plastic face Pucknis.

As soon as the nurse left, Bill ranted. "Worse than any hangin' judge I ever went before. Every time I object to something, she overrules me."

Faith held his hand. "She just wants you to get better."

Bill said, "Shit! After all the trouble we went through to get that meeting, and then my ticker up and spoiled it."

"Bill, we're just glad that you made it through as well as you did."

"It'll be a week or so before I get out. Then they want me to take a month off. But the first thing on my calendar when I get back into the office is rescheduling that meeting."

Faith said, "Bill, don't worry about it."

He looked from Scott to Faith. "Faith, you're not telling me something. You know, I once called this guy foolish. Do I need to say the same about you?"

"Yes, I guess you do. We're a matched pair of fools."

"Well, I'll be damned. You went ahead and met with that pernicious perp Parnelli, didn't you?"

"Yes."

"And what happened?"

"It was fine. Now that's all we're going to tell you. We promised the doctor we wouldn't talk business. Everything went fine, and when you're back in the office, we'll let you in on the whole meeting."

The head nurse marched in. "Okay, this consultation is over."

When they got home from the hospital, Faith was laughing softly.

"What's funny?"

"Come here, you big dumb fool, and give me a kiss."

"Look who's calling who a dumb fool."

THEY HAD COPIED the medical records and overnighted the originals to Jeremy's doctors in Springfield. A week later they got a response, which boiled down to "inconclusive." Faith was more than a little irritated, and called the doctor. "Do you know the troubled waters we navigated to get those records?"

"Sorry, but we need all the information we can get to base our diagnosis and treatment."

"And these records were useless?"

"No, actually they were helpful. As far as they went. At least there seems to be no hereditary renal abnormality in the father and his parents."

"As far as they went?"

"Well, we need records of siblings of the father's parents, too."

"Would that be helpful?"

"Sure. Of course, maybe it would only be a negative result, like the ones you gave us, in other words, ruling out a genetic predisposition toward renal failure."

Faith told Scott, "After all we did..., and I met the devil Doug, and it was all for nothing!"

Scott shook his head. "It's a crap shoot. You never know. Don't blame the doctors. They're just following the textbook. The more medical history you have, the better prepared you are to treat the patient. And you must have helped them pursue a more aggressive course of medication."

"Hi, Faith, it's Addie."

"Great to hear from you. What's up?"

"I know you're real busy, you and Scott, but we're planning a weekend trip to Chi-town, and if you've got time we'd like to stop by."

"Hey, you're staying with us. It would be wonderful to see you, and for the guys to meet."

Faith knew she could count on Scott. He wrangled some box seats for a Cubs game on Saturday afternoon. That gave the girls some time for hen talk. Faith decided she had to bring Adeline up to date on Doug, giving it to her as briefly as possible.

Adeline said, "That no-good, low-down skunk."

"Skunk, rat, snake. Pick your favorite vermin."

"Ya know, before Mike started his business, I worked for a while in a nails place, and we had a treatment for tomcats like Doug."

"Nails?"

"No, when one of the gals told us her man was cheating on her, we said instead of a manicure or a pedicure, the guy needed a testicure."

Faith smiled. "Hmm, I can't imagine what that'd be."

"Yeah, snip off his testicles. De-nut him."

Listening to Adeline's throaty snarl, seeing the fire in her eyes, Faith was transported back to the rough and tumble days of the Alternative High School. Faith didn't like smutty language, "potty talk," but found herself carried away by Adeline's reversion to teenage recklessness. She couldn't resist saying what she ordinarily would have kept to herself: "You mean give him a ballectomy?"

Adeline exploded in a belly laugh. "Damn straight! Hell of a lot better than a vasectomy. Not just stop him from making babies. Turn that bull into a steer, keep him from bothering the cows."

"Well, you're more than thirty years too late, but you sure would have saved a lot of women a bundle of grief. And he still seems to be up to his old ways, so better late than never."

Adeline gave Faith her trademark bear-hug. "I told you back in high school you could make good. And I'm rootin' for you now. Hang in there, baby. Don't let him get away with nothin'."

Faith shed a few tears. "You've always been there for me Adeline. Sorry I couldn't level with you earlier. It was just too complicated."

"Hi, Stan, it's Doug."

"Hi, Doug. So....?"

"So I went to Chicago."

"And?"

"And I met with her. The lawyer didn't show. Got detained or something."

"Hard to believe. Something drastic must have prevented him from meeting with the two of you. I can't believe he'd let his client face you alone."

"Hey, I'm not that hard to take."

"So did the meeting satisfy you?"

"No, not that much. Actually, I do remember her. Met her in a pizza place. She was a knockout then, and is still attractive."

"Always on the prowl, huh?"

"She's not bad. But the downer is, she wouldn't talk. Wouldn't open up. I did most of the talking."

Stan asked, "So what's new?"

"What's new?"

"Yeah, Doug, don't you always do most of the talking?"

"No, I mean, I asked her lots of things, and she just ducked my questions."

"You expected her to be an open book?"

"No, but you know, she even accused me of being selfish."

Stan snickered. "She did? Why would she do that?"

"Well, I admitted I'd been a bad boy, and done some selfish things, and she said yeah, holding up the records for personal reasons was selfish."

"If the shoe fits...."

"Hey, I don't have to take crap from you, too."

"No, you don't, and I don't need any from you. I would like to see some green rather than some brown."

"I'll pay you off, don't worry about it."

"You'll have a little more time, and then if we have to, I'll see you in court. On the other side of the table."

"Well, counselor, before you start suing me, give me some of your legal know-how on what you've already done for me. That paper I signed, it said I would give them medical records for me, my parents, and their siblings."

"Uh-huh. That's what you gave them, her, didn't you?"

"Not exactly."

"You said you had them."

"Well, for me and my folks."

"But not for the others?"

"No. Too much trouble."

"You're a real piece of work. The last thing I was going to do before we traveled to Chicago was make sure you had the goods with you. I can tell you this, that once I knew you didn't have the promised papers, I wouldn't have gone with you even if you'd paid off your account in full. That's a breach of contract, Doug."

"Where does that put me?"

"Behind the eight ball."

"And?"

"And if they want to take you to court, they can."

"Well, that's all I wanted to know. Thanks for the advice."

"While we're on the phone, I'll put it straight to you. You'll be getting a letter from me. Either you start making payments on your account, at least $500 a month until it's paid off, or I have to go to court. Then on top of my bill, you'll have another lawyer to pay."

"$500 a month?"

"You said months ago you'd pay me $2500, so $500 should be chicken feed."

"You take my chicken feed and turn it into chicken shit?"

Simon hung up.

CHAPTER 25

*S*ometimes Scott went to church with Faith. Most of the time she attended alone. As a member, she participated in the mass, taking the body and blood of Christ. Before she joined, she said it didn't make any difference being in church and not taking part in the mass, because she liked just communing with God. But after she joined, she found it made a real difference.

She still communed with God at times, especially overlooking the lake. But the Eucharist was different. One evening when they were relaxing in their recliners, she explained it to Scott. "I know your church background is a little different, but for me, in the Eucharist, God becomes a part of my life. I value that immensely. It makes me realize I am not an independent entity, a self-sufficient being. It reminds me I am the child of God. I owe Father Whitmore a lot, for guiding me through my spiritual problems, and helping me grow in the church. My own father destroyed my childhood religious belief, but Father Whitmore and Harriet Beecher Stowe helped me get right with God."

Scott said, "What you tell me about Father Whitmore reminds me of my Dad. I don't like all the super-religious church members, like your own father, but a lot of ministers and priests are the salt of the earth."

The Sunday after Faith met Doug, she went to church by herself. She didn't have a chance to talk to Father Whitmore, but at the door after the service, he gripped her hand and didn't let go. "We need to talk."

"Sure."

"Tuesday. You leave me a voice mail for the time."

Monday she cleared a half day personal leave, and left a message for the good father that she'd see him at ten. She would miss the rush hour traffic, and could be back in the office before one.

"FATHER WHITMORE, good to see you again. How are you?"

"Fine. Bring me up to date on all your shenanigans."

"Shenanigans! Is that what you call people's problems. No, you first. The last time I talked to you, you seemed to be having a rough period. If you don't want to talk about it, okay, but do I sense things are better?"

"Yes, you caught me traveling a bumpy road. I had to stop and take care of business at home."

"Was I part of the problem? When you met me for lunch?"

"That was the point where the cup overflowed."

"Sorry."

"Not your fault. My wife had been wanting me to take her to lunch in the loop, and I'd been putting it off, and then I went with a parishioner but didn't have time to do it with her."

"Terrible!"

"Uh-huh. I've cut back on my office hours, and we agreed to set aside some quality time every week."

"That's great."

"Now you."

She filled him in on the roller coaster emotional ride leading up to the unexpected solo meeting with Doug.

"You finally did actually meet him, not just see him?"

"Yes."

"And I guess you had some unfinished business to take care of there, right?"

"Well, it was much easier for me than I expected. For a while after I saw him in Peoria, I hated him. Then when I heard about his abysmal personal life, and especially as he himself gave me such a dismal view of his career, I actually pitied him."

"Why?"

"He's pathetic. A loser. And still so hung up on himself he can't see beyond his own skin."

"Did you forgive him?"

"He asked me that, and I said the words. To be honest, I don't know if I really meant it. But I guess he accepted it."

"So his unfinished business is now finished?"

"I hope so. I never want to see him again."

"Well, how's the rest of your life?"

"Wonderful. Our family is such a pleasure. Scott and I get along well. Work goes fine, as usual. Prayer is a part of my daily life. I prayed at bedtime as a child, and I've reestablished that pattern."

"Whatever works for you."

"Well, my dear sainted Father, not just for me. The suggestion you gave me about an 'ecumenical' prayer worked in our family prayer circle, and Rachel, you know she's Jewish, even Rachel chipped in with her prayer for divine assistance in solving our problems."

"That's terrific!"

"I had the support of a lot of people these past few months, but prayer was a stabilizing force for me."

Father Whitmore ended their session with one of his wonderful prayers. She still had the mini recorder with her, something she'd kept in her purse since the Doug meeting, and she turned it on. She wanted to hear it again at home. She didn't want to steal his thunder, just borrow his heaven.

CHAPTER 26

Melanie and Jeremy said it was their turn to host the family, so they set up a weekend reunion at Springfield. Jon and his tribe drove down Friday night. Scott had to take care of weekend papers, so he and Faith headed out of Chicago early Saturday morning.

Faith was in good spirits. "So, Grandpa Scott, what new trick do you have up your sleeve for the kids this time? You've done the newspaper a number of times, then the radio broadcast when we didn't have Jon's computer set-up, and after that the television show."

"You'll see. I think you'll like it."

"I know you were fooling around, putting a box of things in the trunk."

"Hey, no fair peeking."

"I didn't think you'd ever get loaded up. And did you have to clean out your closet today?"

"You know me, Mr. Tidy Closet."

"You're up to something, I just don't know what."

"Even if you saw my stuff, I don't think you'd get it."

"No, but I bet the kids are going to love it."

When they got to the Goodmans, the kids were all at a nearby playground, so Scott got in the house without the kids seeing what Faith called his mystery box. Melanie started to ask Scott what he had, and Faith joked, "Don't go there."

As soon as the kids returned from the playground they descended upon Grandpa Scott. Now they had a menu, and besieged him with a barrage of overlapping questions: "We gonna do a newspaper? A radio broadcast? A television show?"

Scott knew how to gently tease them, and they ate it up.

"Well, I don't know. Are you sure you want to do something?"

They yelled a unanimous affirmative.

"Well, let's see. Raise your hand if you want to do a newspaper."

Mark raised his hand, and when the others were slow on the uptake, he yelled, "Raise your hands!"

Scott looked them over. "Okay, this is a democracy, so we'll vote. How many want to do a radio show? Raise your hand if you want to do a radio show." Mark again got his and other hands in the air.

"I see. Now let's vote on who wants to do a television show."

Now the kids were with it, elevating their hands without any prompting from Mark. But he was the juvenile spokesman. "So what are we gonna do, Grandpa Scott?"

"Well, it looks like a tie to me. You all want to do a newspaper. And you all want to do a radio broadcast. And you all want to do a television show. Is that right?"

"Yeah!"

"Well, okay, if that's what you want. I was going to do something new, something different with you, but if you want to do a newspaper or something, it's okay with me."

Beth cooed, "Something neeeww?"

Mark chimed in, "Wow, you got something new?"

"Yes."

Stephie wanted in the action. "What is it?"

"Not newspaper. Not radio. Not television."

The adults were enjoying the show as much as the kids, intrigued by the banter.

"Kids, do you know at one time there was no electricity? No electric lights, not even any batteries."

Mark said, "You mean back when there were dinosaurs?"

"Well, not quite that far back. But people had fun even then. They told stories."

Stephie volunteered, "I like stories."

"Do the rest of you like stories?"

They nodded.

"Well, we can do a story. We can act it out."

Mark frowned. "What story?"

"Your story. Whatever story you make up."

"How do you make up a story?"

"Oh, it's easy. I'll show you. I brought some friends with me, and they'll help us."

He brought in the large cardboard box from the garage. He had cut a large section out of one side, and draped and stapled a towel over it like the curtain of a theater. He placed the box on one edge of a coffee table so that he could sit on the floor behind the table and use the box as a puppet theater. Then he had the kids close their eyes, because the friends he brought along were a little shy. He quickly inserted his hand in a white sock with a painted face and positioned himself behind the table. Then he told the kids to open their eyes, and had Mark lift the curtain.

"Hi. I used to be a sock. But Grandpa Scott gave me a face. Now I'm a puppet. And I can talk. And I can sing. Mi-mi-mi-mi. Doe-re-mi-fa-so-la-ti-doe."

Scott continued the patter, closing his remarks with an invitation.

"Grandpa Scott brought along a lot of my friends, but they don't have any faces. And if you boys and girls paint faces on them, then these socks will be able to talk and sing like me."

Scott resumed a standing position, produced a large box of markers, and each parent helped a child create a colored face on a white sock. Then each kid had a turn performing. When the kids faltered, not knowing what story to tell, Scott encouraged them to make up any story they wanted to.

Even the adults entered into the action, after they had all the kids up and acting with a personalized sock puppet. Melanie and Rachel got Faith to join them in creating some more artistic versions than the basic eyes-nose-mouth model the kids were using.

Jon and Jeremy made identical faces, and sitting side by side in the theater pit, did a funny skit where the puppets argued back forth which one was Jon, which one was Jeremy. Then the puppets asked the audience to decide the identity of the puppets. The kids went crazy, crawling under the table to see who was seated on the left and right, then sticking their heads above the table to tell who was who. But the twins twisted and interlocked their hands to confuse the kids.

When Faith got Scott out of earshot of the young ones, she whispered to him, "I used to think you were a big dumb fool, but now I see you're just a dumb old sock."

The cardboard puppet theater kept the kids occupied most of the day. Mark and Beth claimed the new device as theirs, since it was on their home territory. But Scott assured Stephie and little Jeb that he'd make a theater for them the next time he came to Oak Park. And he passed on a tip to the moms. "When they get tired of the sock puppets, go to the hardware store and buy the cheapest white canvas gloves you can find. That way you can paint five tiny faces on each finger, and each kid can have a five-actor troupe on one hand."

Lunch had been delayed by the puppet theater, but no one minded. After the meal Rachel managed to put Jeb down for a nap, and the kids were given video time, allowing Scott a break from them.

The adults formed the family prayer circle. Faith ended her prayer with "thanks to you, Lord, for this wonderful family."

Rachel added, "And we pray for your continued protection in the future."

Melanie said, "Faith, I'd like to offer a prayer, too."

"Sure."

"Our Father in Heaven, guide us and give us direction as we seek to do thy will."

Jeremy and Jon looked at each other, not knowing whether to leave this an all-female prayer ensemble, or whether to turn it into an all-family group. The moment passed, and the women dropped their hands, dissolving the circle.

They reconvened around the table, eager to hear Faith recount her meeting with the twins' father.

"It's not the way we planned it, it just worked out that way. It's embarrassing to talk about it, but the best way to sum it up, I guess, is that he's pathetic, a pitiful man. He doesn't have much of any contact with his ex-wives, and his live-in girlfriend left him and took their child. I don't know about the paternity suit from 1982, but suspect that he has more ghosts in the closet. And he claimed he wanted to meet me to apologize...for the past. I didn't say much, just let him talk. But when he tried to pull his religious conscience argument on me, I almost lost it. He said he'd been selfish in the past, and now he wanted to do the right thing. I told him that he was being selfish now, putting his personal demand for a meeting ahead of his own child's need for medical records."

Jeremy jumped in, "You said he had a religious change?"

"Claims he got saved in a meeting, it changed him."

"How?"

"He says he's taking responsibility for his life, but all I can see is that he always worshiped himself, and now he's just found religious justification for his self-centered adulation."

The others laughed.

Jon asked, "You didn't tell him—"

"No, don't worry. I didn't divulge anything, not even whether this 'child' is male or female. He wanted more information, but I gave him nothing. No names, addresses, phone numbers. Not even the fact that you're twins. I know you two guys are adults, and can make your own decisions. But I honestly think it would not be wise to contact him. He's a disaster, he's made a mess of his life, and I think he'd disturb your families if you let him in."

Scott had been quiet, but invoked his "Nose of the camel in the tent." Then he amended his statement. "Except I think he's a different animal, one that brays."

Jon ventured another question, mindful that Melanie and Rachel were protective of their fellow female. "Mom, I just want to get clear, why he didn't give you all the medical records, and are you going to pursue it?"

"He said he was too busy, I'd guess too lazy. And we'll have to wait until Bill Ludwig gets back in the office to see if we're going to go after more medical records. Jeremy's doctors say it could be inconclusive, but they want more records, to rule out a genetic predisposition."

Melanie and Rachel exchanged glances. Melanie brought the curtain down. "Well, that's enough Q and A for today. Let's check on the kids and their video."

Jon hung back and had a chance for a few minutes with Faith.

"Mom, I want to ask you quickly about something. And to be upfront with you, you know I'm always tinkering with Digirel."

She laughed. "Sure, I remember, even my name-dropping of Confucius in that Corporate Leaders conference got you to thinking about the Chinese sage, and that earned him a place in your program."

"Right. But what impressed me lately is the power of your prayers. And it makes me realize I haven't put anything in Digirel dealing with prayer. Where did you come up with this stuff?"

She gave him a quick rundown of Father Whitmore's prayer plan of prayer to, through, and for. Jon was busy tapping away on his handheld, until Rachel saw him, and crossed her arms in an X, saying, "Ixnay on business during family time." He chuckled and obligingly put away his electronic toy.

Faith got in a parting shot, "You should talk to Father Whitmore."

CHAPTER 27

Faith and Scott headed out late Sunday afternoon, after a lengthy session of puppet theater, with each kid acting out his or her favorite story.

Faith gushed, "Scott, you're dangerous! Give you a cardboard box, a bunch of old socks, and a few markers, and you could start a children's revolution. I've never seen kids so energized. And it's not the props, it's you!"

He lit up like a Christmas tree. "Aw, shucks, ma, it was nothin'."

She laughed out loud.

He changed the subject. "Hey, what were you and your smart phone jockey doing after the prayer circle?"

"Believe it or not, he wants to incorporate some prayer stuff into his Digirel program."

"He's more dangerous than I am. If he had a meeting with the pope, he'd cram the whole Catholic church into that handheld."

Their conversation rambled. Faith said, "I was impressed with Rachel and Melanie both contributing prayers."

"Well, Faith, we have to decide whether we'll pursue the medical records, once Bill Ludwig returns to work."

"Oh, Scott, I'm too tired to talk anymore." She shifted around in her seat so she could stretch her hand out on his shoulder as she leaned against him and took a nap.

TWO WEEKS later they were Bill Ludwig's first appointment after his attack.

"Come in, come in. I don't know what I'm going to do with you two. Scott, you do all the detective work for us, and Faith, you handle the negotiations. The firm could make a joint offer, one of you run research, the other public relations and negotiations."

Scott said, "We'll keep the offer in mind."

Ludwig nodded. "The only unfinished business is the incomplete medical records. And to be honest, I kind of dropped the ball there. When Simon faxed me the note saying he no longer represented Parnelli, I was all concerned with keeping the meeting on. What we should have been doing, is discussing the quid pro quo. I already had my script ready, so to speak. I was going to ask him flat out if he had the papers. In other words, papers for the meeting. Then, when he didn't say anything about the papers, I just assumed that Parnelli had them. Lawyers aren't supposed to make assumptions. They should make damn sure and double sure."

Faith wondered, "Where does that leave us now?"

"Frankly, in a pickle. If you think the papers are important, we can pursue it. Ask Parnelli to give us the papers, and if he doesn't, we can take him to court."

"Would it be hard?"

"Faith, my dear, court is never easy. One of the main things is, it would take a lot of time."

"What do you propose?"

"The first thing I'm going to do is call Simon. I owe him a call. Because he drew up the agreement, and his client welshed on it. Even if he doesn't represent the creep any more, it will look bad for his name to be dragged through a breach of contract case."

"Okay. Let us know what you hear."

~

"HELLO, STANLEY. IT'S BILL LUDWIG."

"Uh, yes. I guess you're calling about Doug Parnelli, and I'm still not representing him."

"Yes, so you told me. This isn't new business, it's old business. The agreement you drew up and Parnelli signed."

"Yes, what about it?"

"He didn't perform."

"He did hand over his medical records, didn't he?"

"Yes. His and his parents', but not those of his parents' siblings."

"Uh, yeah. Sorry about that."

"Yes. You're sorry about it. I'm sorry. And so is my client. Is Parnelli sorry?"

"I don't know. I don't represent him and haven't been in contact with him."

"Well, I'd think you would be concerned that an agreement you drew up and forwarded was not fulfilled."

"I wish there was something I could do, but I'm not his attorney."

"Okay, Stanley, I'm going to cut through the polite language. If you think you and Parnelli are getting away with this breach of agreement, you're dead wrong. The only reason the lines didn't burn up with a hot call from me the day of the meeting is that I was in the hospital. And since then I've been under strict doctor's orders not to handle any business. But I made a commitment to myself and my client, that the first thing I would take care of when I got back in the office was to call you. And I'd hoped you would be helpful. And now I hear this whiney 'I'm not his attorney' bullshit.

"That makes me mad, Stanley, and I'm going to go right to the bottom line. If you don't do something with your former client, then I'll do my damnedest to bring you up on charges before the Illinois bar. And don't start sputtering about me making the charges stick. I don't care if they stick or not, just bringing you up on charges would be enough to cut your practice in half. If they wanted to they could disbar you, and your law degree diploma would be toilet paper. Used toilet paper. Now, have I given you sufficient motivation to get on the phone and talk to your former client?"

"Well, I don't know...."

"Stanley, you can stick that phone up your ass, or you can use it to call Parnelli. If you don't call him, you might as well rectalize it, because your sorry asshole will be in the hands of the ethics committee. Now it will take me about twenty seconds to look up the number of the Illinois Bar Association. That's the amount of time you have to reconsider your position."

"Well...sure. I'll call and talk to him...see what I can do."

"Let me be specific: our agreement was for the medical records of Parnelli, his parents, and their siblings. That's what you can do for me. Thank you, Stanley. Nice talking to you."

"DOUG. STAN HERE."

"Hi, Stan. Long time."

"Yeah, Doug, we need to talk."

"Sure, I'll be getting some payments to you. Boy, business has sure been slow."

"The payments we can settle later. We need to talk about the agreement you signed."

"What agreement? I sign a lot of stuff."

"The Chicago agreement. For medical records."

"I handed it over. You wouldn't go, so I had to go myself."

"You know what I mean. Don't screw around with me. The agreement was not just for you and your folks, but all of your parents' brothers and sisters."

"That's a pain, man. What do they need that for, anyway?"

"You know. For medical background."

"Well, let them dig it up, then."

"That's not the point. You signed an agreement to get the records and deliver them if the woman would meet with you. They performed and you didn't. That's breach of agreement."

"So what? They gonna sue me?"

"They may."

"You gonna represent me?"

"We'll handle that when it comes up."

"We're back to the money, huh."

"No, Doug, this isn't just about money. Their hotshot attorney may bring me up on ethics charges."

"What's that?"

"I drew up the papers, you signed them, I forwarded them. So indirectly I was responsible for that meeting. Even if I wasn't at the meeting, the fact that I told their lawyer you would show up at the meeting with the papers puts me on the hook, too. You told me you had the papers, and I took your word for it. So if you don't come across with the papers, he can charge me with bad faith negotiations, the fact that we never had the papers to begin with."

"What do they do to you?"

"Well, it could lead to a reprimand."

"What's that?"

"A bad mark on my record. But just bringing me up on charges would be a black mark itself."

"Stanley, sounds like you should get yourself a lawyer. A good lawyer."

"Don't try to be funny with me, Doug."

"You don't want jokes? What do you want?"

"Those medical records!"

"Well, I'll see what I can do. It would take time."

"How many brothers and sisters did your parents have?"

"My mom had a sister, Aunt Sara. My dad had a brother and a sister."

"That shouldn't be too hard. I've still got some of the blank medical forms for you to fill out."

"Not that simple."

"Why?"

"I haven't kept in touch with my cousins."

"Well, get in touch! Because if you don't hand over those records, it's not just my ass that'll be in a sling. When I talked to their lawyer a few minutes ago, he was furious. The only reason you got away with handing over part of the records is he had a medical emergency that day, and has been recuperating. Now that he's back, he thinks we tricked him, which you did. And he's madder than hell. Even if his client doesn't come after us, he'll make both of us pay. He has the money and the connections, and he'll fry both of us."

"Okay, okay, I'll try to get the records."

CHAPTER 28

"Father Whitmore, it's good to see you again."

"Glad to see you, Faith."

"Gee, I'm always coming to you with my problems. Let me at least start out today asking how things are with you."

"Fine."

"You know I'm concerned about things at home, because I realize all your time with me took you away from...your wife."

"We patched things up, and now that we've set aside some quality time each week, she's a lot more comfortable with my commitment to the parish." He chuckled. "Now she knows I'm committed to her as well as to the church."

"Great! Do you ever socialize with parishioners?"

"Our ministerial alliance advises us against that. Playing favorites with certain members. But if you're fishing for whether we'd accept an invitation, consider it a done deal. I think you'd enjoy meeting my wife, and I'd like to get to know Scott. Maybe we can even influence him into coming to church with you more often."

"I'm glad to hear that. We're in the midst of heavy duty negotia-tions right now, but when we get past that, we'll think about something at our place."

"What's the problem now?"

She brought him up to date on the dealings with Doug.

"You're not mad at him now?"

"No. He's such a creep. A pathetic pile of...."

"Was that anger I just heard?"

"Well, you know, when our half hour was up in the restaurant, he blocked my path and wouldn't let me out of the booth. I had to threaten to call the manager and have him thrown out. Does that give me the claim to some indignation?"

"Not good behavior."

"Lousy behavior. And he's so self-centered. But let's get to the bottom line here. I told my twins that I thought they shouldn't contact him. They can decide on their own, but I think he's such a mess himself that he'd just ruin the twins' lives. Sure, I'm selfish here. He'd ruin my life and my family's harmony. But you know, the kids are bonded to Grandpa Scott and Grandma Faith, and introducing him would upset the apple cart."

"Uh...Faith, you're feeling guilty for depriving him of access to his own kids?"

"I guess so. You're always good at smoking me out. I don't deny it. But my executive/manager/professional head says the guilt is irrelevant. The point is that this guy has destroyed several families and relationships and who knows how many women's lives, so why should he even have the option of ruining our happy haven?"

"You've got a point. He doesn't have a good track record."

"He claims to have been saved, reborn. But I can't see it. Just a religious version of his myopic concern. Now that he's alienated himself from those close to him, he wants to feel good by getting close to us. I see another Titanic heading for the iceberg, and I don't want our family to be with him on that voyage."

"You have a colorful way of putting it."

"What can you tell me about reborn people? Are they legit?"

"Yes and no. Everyone's heard about the death row inmates who get religion. And I'm not against it, but you've got to wonder how genuine the conversion is if a person is faced with execution."

"Father, I'm not the one to judge Doug. Only God can judge him, I know. But that's in the other world. I'm here, in this world, and I've waited thirty years to get together with my flesh and blood. I can't describe to you the joy it brings me. When I pray at night, that's what I thank God for, bringing me back together with them. And I want to protect them. You can't blame me for that, can you?"

"No."

"Well, I guess if I was Catholic, I'd say 'Bless me Father, for I have sinned.' If it's a sin to keep our identity from Doug, refuse his requests, then maybe it's a sin I'll have to live with."

"You did forgive him?"

"Yes. He asked for it, I gave it, so I provided him his absolution."

"But you haven't worked it out in your heart?"

"No, and I'm using your lessons, like I did with my dad. Forgiveness is a process, takes time. I completed the course with my father. Now I'm mid-course with Doug. Well, maybe just in the beginning stage."

"Then if you're refusing Doug access to the family, out of concern for them, and not out of bitterness or hatred toward him, how can that be a sin?"

"I think, Father Whitmore, you have just granted me my absolution."

He made the sign of the cross and said, "Go in peace."

She smiled. "One more thing, Father. I don't want to take up a lot of your time. You and this church have been a real Godsend to me. And I mean that literally. I've been thinking of the right thing to do, and have a suggestion."

"Yes."

"I was thinking of a stained glass window. That would have to be approved by your building committee, wouldn't it?"

"Yes, that's the procedure. What did you have in mind?"

"What I would like is not going to pass their review. I'd like to commission a window for Harriet Beecher Stowe."

He chuckled, "Non imprimatur."

"What?"

"Latin for not permitted, you know, not approved or sanctioned."

"So the B plan is what you might explore with them. A stained glass window of Mary. Maybe a Madonna. Mary and child. What do you think?"

"Some in the church might consider it too Catholic, but that's part of our Episcopal heritage, too. I'll run it by them."

"Let me know what they think, and then we could explore how much it would cost. And, keep it anonymous."

CHAPTER 29

"Stan, Doug."

"Hi, Doug. Do you have the records?"

"Getting right to the down and dirty, huh?"

"For the best interests of both of us, we need to get this resolved, pronto."

"Well, good news for both of us. I got hold of my cousins, and they gave me the basic information on the health, sickness, and cause of death for my folks' siblings."

"Good. You can send or bring it to my office, and I'll send it on to Ludwig's office so he can pass it on."

"Hold on a minute, you're getting the cart ahead of the horse. Or the papers ahead of the meeting."

"What meeting?"

"Remember? Last time I handed the papers over in person. No, you don't remember, cause you didn't attend the party. Just me and Faith."

"Cut the monkey business, Doug. You're in over your head. Just because you got out of that meeting alive means nothing. Quit being cute and let me have the papers."

"No dice. No meeting, no papers."

"Holy shit!"

"No shit. That's the way it's gonna be. So pass the word to the Chi-town folks."

"You know I'm not representing you anymore."

"Well, Stan, Fiji buddy, I think you got no choice. You have no papers, you face the ethical commission or whatever."

"That's blackmail!"

"No, Stan, I'm learning this lawyer game. It depends on who has what. I have something you want, so you dance to my tune."

"You know what I think of you?"

"You don't have to tell me. I can guess. For the moment, just consider me a good negotiator. Now here's the terms. A meeting. Sure, I know, I call the shots for the meeting, so they get home turf in Chicago. But this time to Hell with Faith. She's a mean lick. I want to meet with my kid. Hand the papers over to the kid who's gonna benefit from them."

"You're crazy!"

"You know, if I was a jazz musician, that'd be a compliment. Crazy, man." Now I've got to earn some money, so call me when you have a meeting confirmed. Otherwise, I'm not interested in talking to you."

~

"HELLO, BILL, THIS IS STAN SIMON."

"Hello, Stan. I hope you have good news for me."

"Well, I have some good news and some not so good news."

"Give me the good news, Stanley, make me happy."

"I have the records."

"That is good news. Now don't spoil the good news. Don't make me too unhappy with the bad news."

"Parnelli wants to hand over the materials in person."

"That's not good, not good at all. Haven't we played this scene before?"

"Yes. I tried to talk him out of it, but he wouldn't budge."

"Let's get something straight here. Are you his legal counsel?"

"Not really."

"Hmm. 'Not really.'" Can you parse that for me in legalese? Are you going to represent him if this goes through the courts?"

"I don't know."

"Well, you better make your mind up, because this might move very quickly."

"I'll level with you."

"Please do."

"He's got me over a barrel. He knows you might take me before the ethics review board if we don't hand over the records."

"You...told him that?"

"Yes, I—"

"Bad move, Stan, you gave him the leverage, and now he's using it."

"I guess you're right, I shouldn't have told him."

"So he's blackmailing you."

"That's about it."

"Alright. Let's talk, just you and me. Forget about clients for the minute. What are your intentions?"

"I'm going to try to get you the papers, and settle this once and for all. As soon as possible."

"Fine. Glad to hear that, Stan. Now let's talk about this meeting foolishness. I understand from my client he didn't behave well in the restaurant. After the agreed upon half hour, he tried to keep her from leaving. Stood in her way and insisted on talking more with her, even meeting his kid. She had to threaten to call the manager and have him ejected."

"What?"

"Yes, did Parnelli fail to tell you that?"

"He didn't say anything about it."

"Well, my client underwent one unpleasant encounter with your client, under duress, I might add, so she's not likely to accept another invitation."

"He doesn't want to meet with her...your client. He wants to meet his kid."

"This is moving from the ridiculous to the ludicrous."

"I tried to talk him out of it, but he's stubborn."

"Let me point something out. We already established he's blackmailing you. Now he's blackmailing my client, and you are a party to it."

"I don't like it. It stinks. But either way, I lose. If I don't get you the records, I'm up before the bar. If I go along with him to have a meeting, using the papers as blackmail, I risk collusion with a devious scheme."

"Stan, if you don't realize it, you're stuck between slimy shit and a hard turd."

"I'll work with you to do what I can, but I've known this guy since college, and don't think he'll back down."

"Okay, here's my plan. You tell Parnelli his withholding what he owes us is blackmail, and see if he backs off. I'll run the meeting by my people. Oh, yes, Stan."

"Yes."

"Don't jerk me around on this. I'm just beginning to like you. But if you get cute and try to double-cross me, I'll see that you never father any more children."

"I understand."

"Be sure that you do. You know that phrase liar, liar, pants on fire? Well, now it's lawyer, lawyer, pants on fire. If you dick around and lie to me this time, your pants will be on fire. I'll burn your buns and roast your genitals."

"You don't have to threaten me. I'm not lying."

"You better not be. You know, my retirement is set. I can quit tomorrow and live comfortably. If I have to, I can spend the first months of my leisure time watching the bar association hang you out to dry and swing in the wind. That's something to keep in mind as you deal with that perp Parnelli."

∾

"FAITH. BILL LUDWIG."

"How are you doing?"

"Well as can be expected. Don't have as much pep as I used to. And I have a Peoria report. Not all bad but not all good."

"Let me have it."

"Simon says they have the records, but Parnelli wants to hand them over."

"You mean—"

"Not to you, but to his child."

Faith didn't reply.

"Faith? Are you there?"

She said, "That's not fair!"

"It's blackmail."

"What did you tell Simon?"

"That he and his frat buddy are on dangerous ground. Blackmail. And that I'd pass on the request to you."

"Give me a quick read."

"Simon is on our side. He's running scared because I told him I could take him before the bar ethics board for reneging on the records. Simon goofed, told Parnelli about the ethics charges, and now Parnelli is using it against Simon, refusing to let him have the records unless he sets up a meeting so Doug can personally hand over the papers."

"Options?"

"Basically, same as before. If you want the papers immediately, the meeting. We can win the court case hands down. But there's an additional disadvantage for any court proceeding: full names and identity."

"Thanks for the summary. I'll run this by Scott and get back to you."

CHAPTER 30

When Scott got home from the newspaper, Faith was waiting for him.

"Scott, Parnelli is a double SOB." She explained the situation. "What do you think?"

"Actually, I'm not so afraid of him as I once was. In fact, I'd feel better if you were meeting him. You stared him down alone, and can handle him. You're strong. But I worry about Jeremy. He's a little vulnerable. Soft. Well, the word I have in mind is 'naive.'"

"You're right, Scott. But the decision isn't ours to make."

"No. I guess it's up to Jeremy. And Melanie."

"And it can affect Jon and his family, too."

She got Jeremy and Jon on a three-way call, explaining the latest development. "Take some time to think it over, and then, if you can, come to the condo this weekend to talk it over."

Scott took the phone from Faith. "Hey, guys, I'd be glad to take the kids for the afternoon, a tour of Chicago. That way you will have the condo to yourselves."

The weekend ushered in a glorious day for Chicago. The two families arrived in good spirits, in spite of the daunting discussion they faced. Faith had a nice lunch prepared for them. The kids were too excited to sit down and eat, fascinated by the condo, especially its mile high (to them) view of the lake. Their mothers had to corral them to sit down at the table.

After lunch, the kids were pestering Grandpa Scott about their special outing with him, but Faith pulled rank and said first she needed Grandpa for a prayer circle. As the older folks joined hands, the younger set pushed their way into the group, holding a parent's hand. Faith gave her usual prayer of thanks for the family and request for guidance in their deliberations.

Rachel tuned in immediately after Faith, voicing an intense plea. "Help us to see what we do not see, Lord. Help us to know what we do not know, Lord." Then she hesitated, and ended the prayer with even greater urgency. "Help us to do what we must do, Lord."

That was Melanie's cue. "Our Father in Heaven, we come together again to take directions. We are weak. We are lost. Help us find ourselves. And each other. Show us the way, and we will follow."

Faith was holding Jon's and Jeremy's hands. Grandpa Scott had been commandeered by the grandkids. And she felt her twin offspring tighten their grip as their spouses invoked higher powers.

They were all relaxing and dissolving the circle when Scott said, "Just a minute. I have a prayer. And I want the boys and girls to pray with me. Dear God, we are so thankful to have Mark, Beth, Stephie, and Jeb in our family. We thank you for this blessing. And we ask you to be with us today and help us find our way, have a happy trip, and return safely. Amen."

The parents and then Mark and Beth repeated the Amen, and Stephie, not to be left out, said, "Amen me too."

The kids had been primed for the outing with Scott before they arrived, so they knew they'd have to mind him. He was sure they'd behave, but he had some ground rules. "First, everybody has to go to the bathroom." Jeb, still in diapers, was changed while the others made their obligatory pit stop. "Next, kiddies, Grandpa Scott needs help on our trip. Mark, will you help me with Beth? And Stephie, will you help me with Jeb? And Beth and Jeb, will you help me with Mark and Stephie?"

The kids shouted an ear-splitting, "Yeah!"

As they ran to the door, excited about their trip, Scott said, "You people have a leisurely talk. Whatever you come up with is fine with me. If you need my input, Faith knows what I think. I'll be back in a couple of hours."

Rachel looked at Jeb with some doubt. "Honey, do you want to go?"

"Yeah!"

"Scott, he'll probably fall asleep."

"We'll handle it. I'd hate to leave him behind and then have him listen to the other kids tell him what they saw and did."

Being a newspaper reporter had its advantages. He had seen an early press release about a Loop tour on a rebuilt double decker bus, an old British model with the upper deck open to the sky, and wrangled tickets for them. He didn't tell the kids in advance, wanting to make sure the weather was good and they could find seats together. First they piled into a taxi and took the short ride to the pickup point for the bus. When the kids saw the huge bus, they went gaga. The lineup saw Scott with four children, and let his kindergroup board first. They clambered up the stairs and got front row seats.

"What happened to the top?" Beth asked.

The tour guide had his banter ready. "We peeled it off with a can opener."

Mark asked, "Where did you get such a big can opener?"

The diesel bus was idling, waiting for the start of the tour.

"It stinks," Stephie announced.

"It's smokey," Scott explained.

"Yeah, that's what I said. It's smokey."

When the old bus lurched on its takeoff, the kids squealed. Jeb, seated in Scott's lap, was scared, and started to whimper, burying his head in Scott's chest. But as soon as he heard the other kids laughing, he grinned and joined them. The hop over the Chicago

River was a thrill. And the trip along the lake was an eyeful. The guide tried to narrate the trip, but they couldn't hear well over the din of the engine and traffic. "This is Shedd Aquarium, otherwise known as the Fishhouse. But don't go there to eat. The fish are only to look at." Scott told the kids that if they wanted to, they might come back to the Aquarium. The children screamed their yes. But Scott told them there were other things they might do, too.

As the tour bus made the mandatory trip past the Sears Tower, the driver announced, "This tower once was the tallest building in the world." Beth asked Scott, "Did it get shorter?" Mark was the young adult, explaining that other taller buildings had been built after this one.

After their tour of the loop, back to their starting point, Scott laid out two possibilities, and they'd have to choose. They could go back to the Aquarium, the "Fishhouse," or they could take a ride on a train. Stephie wanted to know if they'd be home in time for bed. Scott assured them they'd be back in time for supper. They wanted to do both, but Scott made them choose. He explained that to get to the train they'd have to go down in the ground, and then the train would take them above ground, high up. The kids liked that. "The train! The train!"

So Doug led them to a subway station. Buying tokens and going through the turnstile itself was a new experience. Jeb clung to Scott, and he warned the others to hold hands. They sat on seats next to the wall waiting for a train, and when one came in, they rushed on together, finding a bench that would accommodate all of them. Jeb lasted until the train climbed out of its earthen tunnel into the daylight. Then he leaned back on Grandpa Scott and was sound asleep. Scott pointed out Wrigley Field where the Cubs played baseball.

CHAPTER 31

*M*eanwhile, back at the condo, it was time for the big discussion.

Faith felt nervous before the meeting. She had been taken aback by the fervent prayers of Rachel and Melanie. It wasn't what they said, or prayed. It was the intensity of their appeal. After lunch, clearing the table with Melanie and Rachel, she asked them, "Hey, gals, what's up? I can sense some difficulties."

Melanie said, "Don't worry, Mom, it'll be okay." Rachel started to add something, when Jon and Jeremy walked into the kitchen.

Looking into Rachel's and Melanie's eyes, she was reassured. She knew, as in previous family councils, they would be backing her. Protecting her. From her own sons!

She looked at Jeremy and Jon, but their eyes were distant, not revealing their inner feelings. Oh, how she wished Scott was at her side. But she had to forge ahead.

The five were seated around the kitchen table.

Faith said, "I don't know what else there is to say, I've already told you the situation, so let's just hear what you think."

Jeremy jumped in. "Mother, you're not for a meeting, are you?"

"No, not if we can avoid it." She looked anxiously around the table.

"And why not?"

"Nothing is to be gained from a meeting. I mean, except for the records, and we already have an agreement for the records that's been broken."

Jeremy continued, "And Scott is against it, too, right?"

"Well, yes. He thinks like me, that...your father...is unreliable, unpredictable, and there's no telling what trouble he might cause."

There was a lull. Faith spoke up again. "Well, guys, I didn't want to be the one to go first, laying down the law. I wanted to hear what you two thought...and your wives, too."

Before the others could speak, Jeremy turned to her. "Tell us again the advantages and disadvantages."

"Let me put it quickly, the way the lawyer did. For speedy access to the records, choose the meeting. If we don't want a meeting, he's sure a court will get them for us. But a court proceeding would take time, and would mean divulging our names and identities. That's the long and short of it."

Jeremy stumbled. "So...it's not the meeting as such that you two don't like, it's the consequences."

"Right. In fact, if the proposal had been for me to meet and get the papers, Scott would have okayed it this time. Last time, he was totally against it, but since he knows I can handle your father, he'd be more open to that."

Jeremy persisted. "But don't you think I'd be able to handle him?"

"Uh, I didn't mean that. It's just that if you didn't have to meet him, it might be better. The more of our family he meets, the more likely he is to cause trouble."

Jeremy turned to Faith. "And why do you think he'd make trouble?"

"He admits himself that he has, in his own words, messed up several of his own families. And his live-in and child. And who knows how many others."

After another lengthy pause, Faith ventured, "Jeremy, I sense that you're more for a meeting, is that right?"

"I'm not against a meeting. Not in principle. I don't see that it could hurt anything. I meet people all the time, and so he doesn't seem to be a threat."

Jon had been holding his mouth with his hand, but jerked it off. "Threat to who? I mean, to whom?"

Jeremy looked at him. "To me. I'd be meeting him."

Jon countered, "But the rest of the family would be involved. Indirectly."

Jeremy said, "Not necessarily. All he'd have to know is that I'm the child. I'm the one who needs the records, and—"

Jon interrupted. "For now the records are for you, but they'll be important in the future for me and for our kids. I mean, all of our kids."

"Yes, of course, but what I meant was, the reason we're asking him for the records is my medical condition."

"But if he worked his way into our family, it would affect all of us."

"Jon, why do you think that would happen? If Mom could meet with him and get part of the records without revealing our identity, why couldn't I get the rest of the records?"

"Jeremy, don't get me wrong. I don't think either Mom or me is questioning you and your abilities. The person we're questioning is someone who's proven to be unreliable, who might somehow...as Scott said, get his nose in our tent."

Jeremy said, "Well, I don't want to disagree with what some of you are thinking and saying, but I've heard this word 'unreliable' a number of times, and it does bother me. I mean, all of us are imperfect. Sinners. So no one is totally, one hundred percent reliable, all the time. And if that's the case, then why should this one man, our father, be characterized as totally unreliable?"

Jon snorted, shaking his head in disgust. "Jeremy, because he's proven himself to be unreliable. That's what he admits. He says it himself."

"Jon, that's where we may part ways. I look at people not just through their faults and flaws, but also through their potential for redemption. And after all, this man says he's been saved, and is trying to be a better man. I don't see why we can't help him redeem himself. Sure, he's done a lot of bad things, behaved badly. And he admits it. Confesses it. Asks for forgiveness. And is trying to do the right thing, apologizing in person. That doesn't seem so 'unreliable' to me. He seems to be calling out for help. And I don't see why we can't be of help to him. It doesn't mean we're going to take him into our house, feed and clothe him, and be his caretaker. But I think it would be a mistake to shut him out."

Faith's heart pounded. Now she saw clearly what her daughters-in-law had foreseen. And she knew that in this discussion they couldn't cut their husbands short. They had to let their men play out their positions and emotions. She counted on them to come in later and patch things up. For the moment, the issue had to be engaged.

Jon objected, "I beg to differ. This guy has shut himself out. And sorry to disagree with you, but he's a loser who lost two families and a live-in and, like Mom says, who knows how many others. All his own fault. Nobody did him wrong. And after he loses everything, he wants to patch things up with us. Give me a break! Yeah. Give me a break, but not him. He doesn't deserve a break."

"Jon, everyone needs a break."

"Well, I don't need to give it to him."

"Jon, you say he only came to our family after losing everything else. But he didn't even know about us until recently, so it's not as if he thumbed his nose at us for thirty years, and then came crawling back to us."

"Well, he certainly was busy all those thirty years, with at least four other women, probably a lot more."

"Yeah. A classical prodigal son. Or maybe the prodigal father. He's a sinner. But everyone has sinned and fallen short of the glory of God."

Faith had lost control of the meeting. She glanced back and forth at her daughters-in-law. They caught her visual signal and exchanged looks.

Rachel spoke first. "Jeremy, let me ask you this, even if we accept your argument that your father is a sinner in need of help, do you see any point in Jon's argument that there may be some danger involved?"

Jeremy faced her. "Sure, there's danger. In all human relationships there's danger. But it doesn't mean we stop relating to people."

Rachel asked, "Alright, a second question: are we the only ones who can give him help, and do we have to do it in this particular meeting for the records?"

"No, of course not. Anyone can give him help. And you're right, we don't have to give him help in this way at this time in this place. But on the other hand, if everyone in the world had that attitude, it would mean no one would ever help him."

Melanie asked, "Jon, do you see Jeremy meeting your father as much too dangerous, or can the danger be controlled and contained? To put it differently, can we be of some help to your father without him hurting the rest of us?"

"Sure, Melanie, you're right. Meeting with him doesn't mean Jeremy gets killed, or the rest of us gets infected with a terminal disease. Maybe we could give him a boost without too much damage. But the whole scene would have to be, as you put it, very well controlled."

Faith said, "Fellows, you know that Scott and I aren't enthusiastic about a meeting. But we didn't rule it out. To be honest about all this, the first time around, Scott and I had a lot of trouble reaching an agreement. He was adamantly opposed to a meeting, and I was open to it. Only after we'd exhausted all possibilities did he finally agree to a meeting. And the way he agreed was to make sure the situation, the conditions, checked out.

"But let's get back to the present. I hear Jeremy saying he's for a meeting, and willing to see it take place if it's made safe. I hear Jon saying he's against a meeting, but willing to let it take place if it's controlled. Is that a fair assessment?"

Jeremy nodded, "I guess so."

Jon thought a moment, then said, "I'm not for the meeting yet, but not totally against it. Maybe I could accept it if we had the safeguards in place."

Faith said, "Let me help out. It never was the plan for me to meet one-on-one with Doug. And this time, too, we could set the place in Ludwig's law offices, with him and the other lawyer present. How would that be, Jon?"

"Uh-huh. That makes it a lot better. Provides a kind of seat belt to prevent injury."

Jeremy asked, "Jon, what other conditions would you want?"

Jon said, "Well, the single most important principle I have in mind is the game plan Mom carried with her and stuck to in her meeting: no revealing of names, identities, addresses, and so on. I don't know about you, but I don't want this guy knocking on my door, surprising my wife and kids, saying, 'Hi, you don't know me, but I'm grandpa.'"

Jeremy nodded. "You're right, Jon. I don't want any unwelcome, unannounced visitors."

"Yeah, Jeremy, what would happen if he showed up at One Way headquarters?"

"I wouldn't like that."

Melanie and Rachel, having contributed their crucial role as mediators, sat back, content to let the guys think they had reached this middle ground on their own.

The meeting was petering out, and again the women's auxiliary had come to Faith's aid. Rachel spoke for them. "Guys, do you realize that your mother got this place clean, fed us all, and has conducted a heavy duty meeting, and she might be tired? Time to give it a rest."

Melanie said, "I'm going to fix some drinks. Who wants coffee? Tea?"

Faith was relieved. "Guys, why don't you sit in the recliners and enjoy the lake?"

She had tears in her eyes, going to the wives to give and receive hugs. She only said, "Thanks gals. Thanks so much."

THE KIDS EXPLODED into the condo, a torrent of information about where they'd gone, what they'd seen. Scott was still carrying Jeb. "Heavens to Betsy. What've you been feeding this boy? Lead biscuits? He must weight a ton." He added, "I'm only joking, I love every pound of him."

He looked at Faith, and could tell from her face that things were settled. He didn't have to ask for a replay. That could come later. He announced, "I'm springing for dinner, so you people make up your mind where you want to go." And I think we can time it so the children can see Buckingham Fountain light up. We went by in the bus, and I told them we'd try to see it tonight."

To no one's surprise, the juvenile vote was for pizza. Scott told the adults not to despair, because they'd go to Como's, one of the best pizza and Italian places in Chicago. "If it was good enough for your Mom when I was dating her, it should meet your approval." Then he turned to the kids, to include them. "Boys and girls, when we go to this restaurant, watch out, because Al Capone, the big gangster, used to hang out here."

"Who's Owkapone, Grandpa Scott?" Mark asked.

"A gangster."

"Will he be there tonight?"

"Oh, he's dead. He won't be there...but maybe his ghost will."

Faith scolded Scott. "Don't put nonsense in his head. Or scare him."

Scott said, "Grimm's fairy tales couldn't be any grimmer than the glimmer of Al Capone."

They shoehorned themselves into Faith's and Scott's cars for the drive to Como's. The children liked the pizza. The twins and their spouses appreciated the atmosphere as well as the food.

They left Como's full of pizza, pasta, and pop, in a good mood.

First they cruised by Buckingham Fountain. The younger set got so excited that Faith and Scott dropped the families off, drove the two cars back to the condo and parked, and then hoofed it to the fountain. The children were still oohing and aahing as the fountain changed its colors.

The two families went back to the condo to pick up their cars and then head for Oak Park to bed down for the night. The children were disappointed they didn't get to sleep at Grandma and Grandpa's, but there was no room at the condo.

CHAPTER 32

*F*aith collapsed in her recliner, totally exhausted. "Scott, you must be as bushed as I am. Carrying Jeb around all afternoon."

"I'm not that tired. But my lower back is complaining. I'm out of shape. So give me the lowdown on the meeting. I could tell from your face, and the good feelings in the group, that things went well."

"Not so well as you might think from the outcome. It got rather hairy with Jeremy arguing for the meeting, Jon against it, but the gals did a one-two squeeze, each tackling a brother-in-law, and brought them together for a peaceable compromise."

"Which is?"

"Jeremy gets his meeting. Jon gets his conditions, safeguards. About the same thing you and I would go for."

"Great."

"Super. And I can't believe how those two moms handled it. Defused the conflict. Subtly. Gently. Firmly. When they had greased the skids for the compromise, they got out of the way and let the guys slide it into place and take the credit for meeting each other half way."

"Maybe they should work for the State Department, or the U.N."

"I'd be glad to recommend them."

THE NEXT DAY Faith and Scott motored out to Oak Park and took in Brookfield Zoo with the two families. Everyone had a great time viewing the animals through the eyes of the youngsters, especially Jeb, his first zoo experience.

Jeremy and family stayed over Sunday night so that he and Jon could make a ten o'clock Monday appointment with Faith and Scott at Ludwig's office. The brothers drove in, leaving the kids with the womenfolk.

"Well, Scott and Faith, come in. And I'm glad to finally meet these two guys I've been hearing so much about. Have to check my glasses. I'm not seeing double, am I?"

Jeremy and Jon introduced themselves.

"The first thing I want to tell you two is that you have one helluva lady for a mother. Excuse my French, but I can't tell you how lucky you are to have her. And together with Scott, the super sleuth, they make an unbeatable team."

Scott and Faith returned the compliments to Bill for his handling of difficult issues.

"Okay, folks, let's get down to business. I understand, Jeremy and Jon, that you had a family discussion this weekend, and these two brought you up to date on the status of our request for medical records, right?"

Jeremy and Jon nodded.

"Have you reached some decision about the meeting-for-records deal, or do we go to court?"

Jeremy gave the response. "Well, Mr. Ludwig—"

"Bill."

"Okay, Bill. We've kind of made a decision, but before we actually go one way or the other, we'd like to hear how you look at it."

"Of course, that's what I meant, any questions you have I'll handle as best I can. The legal issues I can settle, the personal aspects are more iffy."

Jeremy said, "Yes, and it's the iffy personal issues that concern us most. I guess we're asking what if we have a meeting?"

"Do you want a meeting?"

"We need the records, and a meeting seems to be, according to what you told Mom, the speedy route to them."

"Yes. Definitely. Court would take time. Six months to a year. Minimum."

"Okay...Bill, let's say we go for the meeting...as a quick way to get the records...well, that's the advantage, but both Mom and Scott have warned us about our father, Mr. Parnelli, and...."

"You want me to give you a read on Mr. Parnelli?"

"I guess that's what it boils down to."

"I'm at a disadvantage there. Your mother and Scott are a better source of information than me, because both of them had eyeball to eyeball meetings with him. And I know, from more than thirty years of lawyering, that you won't find a better judge of character than these two people. When they tell me that he's, excuse my frankness, but that serves you best, your father is shifty and undependable, I have to believe them.

"Now mind you, here I'm relaying to you what my two informants have already told you. Nothing new. So what can I add that complements their report? Plenty. I've had to deal with him indirectly through his lawyer, and I talked with him on the phone. And let me just remind you, since this is our first meeting, that the confidentiality rule applies two ways. What you tell me remains confidential. And what I'm going to tell you has to remain confidential. And the reason for that is it's essential to help me protect your interests.

"Well, that's out of the way. Now, what I can tell you about your father, from my dealings with his attorney, is disturbing, to say the least. You know he has had unstable relations with his two families and his common-law arrangement, and in at least one paternity suit. On top of that he's stiffed his lawyer for fees.

"His lawyer refused to represent him, and he is now black-mailing his lawyer into representing him for the meeting, because I scared the Hell out of the lawyer with an unethical behavior charge for not producing the medical records. I don't know if your mother used the word 'blackmail' for his present proposal, but that's what I would call it. Withholding what is ours unless we pay him his ransom, the meeting.

"Let me give it to you straight and simple. He's unreliable, unpredictable, irresponsible. And devious. I've only seen a few clients who were clever enough to outmaneuver and out-negotiate their own lawyers. My only direct contact is talking with him on the phone, but my impression is that he's smart and tricky."

Jeremy hung his head. "You're saying we've got to be careful with him."

"Damn right. Damn careful. He's bright and clever."

Jon chipped in. "Are you saying we shouldn't meet him?"

"No. That's a decision you people, especially Jeremy, need to make. My job here is to help you assess the situation, know the legalities and the options, then choose the one that best suits your preferred time, method, expenditure, privacy, all those concerns, and then execute the choice as effectively as possible."

Jon asked, "So say we did set up a meeting with our father, how would you do it?"

"Well, for one thing, this time I would insist on it being in our offices here. Your mother had a real rough time in that restaurant. We conceded that point the last time, but I wouldn't go along with it again. Sorry, fellows, but Parnelli can't be trusted, and I can't be responsible if we don't meet here. Frankly speaking, and this is most confidential, his lawyer is cooperating with me, so he'll surely advise Parnelli to meet with us."

Jon asked, "What else would you do? What other conditions?"

"Well, another important point is that his lawyer, Simon would have to come. And I'd get a promise from Simon to keep him reined in, control him."

"And?"

"Well, the time would be on our side. That goes along with the turf, our turf. In the restaurant, when your mother met him, Parnelli tried to detain her, and it got dicey. Could have been real bad. I don't think he has a history of violence, but his pattern of social relations is alienating himself from everyone. And alienated people can be desperate. Well, back to the point. At the end of our agreed time, or earlier if he gets nasty, we simply usher him out. We can tell him to leave, or I can call building security. Hate to even think of that, but in the past, especially with some marital disputes, we've had to show some irate guys the door."

Jeremy asked, "Any other precautions or safeguards?"

"Yes. One of the most important, I haven't even mentioned. Last time, because Simon stopped representing Parnelli, and I had my attack, we didn't go over the verification of the records. This time around, I'd insist Simon have a third party look over the records and verify they were up to snuff, then hold them until the meeting took place, and the actual delivery of the goods would be from the third party."

Jeremy said, "I don't see...what's the reason for that?"

"Because I don't trust Parnelli. He stiffed us last time, and I don't like to be beat twice by the same guy with the same stick."

Jeremy asked, "Why do you think he would...cheat us?"

"Simple. Past behavior is the best predictor of future behavior. He cheated us once, so he'd probably cheat us again. If we gave him the chance. We don't want to give him that opportunity, now, do we?"

Jeremy seemed surprised. "Mr. Ludwig—Bill—let me ask a different question. About motive. What we understand as his reason for handing over the documents is he's had a religious change, and is trying to improve himself. Right?"

"That's what he says. At least what his lawyer says that he's been told. And he said as much to me."

"Do you believe him?"

"Who?"

"Mr. Parnelli."

"I have no basis for judging that. That is, the veracity of his religious state of mind. I only know that his actions are devious and unethical. Whether or not he has a conscience, I don't know. And frankly, I don't care. We want the records, and whatever reason he has for delivering them, or withholding them, is no concern of mine, except that knowing about it puts me in a better position for getting you the goods."

"Well, it concerns me. You know I'm a minister."

"Yes, I had forgotten about that. Excuse my rather salty language. It's an occupational hazard of the legal profession. I'll try to watch it."

"Let me ask you again what you think his motive is."

"Well, reverend, you have me there. That's outside my field. I'm not a head doctor or a man of the cloth, so I don't deal with motive. We had some course work on that in law school, but it comes up mainly in criminal law. The difference between voluntary and involuntary homicide. First degree and second degree murder. Did the defendant intend to go to the victim's house and kill him? Well, if he bought a 357 Magnum a week ahead of time, went every day to the woods for target practice on a cutout of a man, and then lay in wait each day for a week outside his house, making sure when the victim returned home, and ambushed him as he got out of his car, we can make the case that the defendant certainly acted as if he intended to kill the guy.

"And if the victim had been having an affair with the defendant's wife, we have a strong argument for what we call motive. After all, motive is what prompts or induces a person to act. As lawyers, we can't photograph motive, we can only infer from actions, and statements, if the guy is stupid enough to make them, what motivates him."

"Yes, Bill, I know what motive is."

"Well, Jeremy, let's pole vault from law to psychology. Freud taught us that surface rationality often masks deeper irrationality, and what passes for rationale often is a masquerade for rationalizing. Basically, you're asking me if Mr. Parnelli is showing his true face or a false face. And I can't be sure enough to tell you which one."

Jeremy leaned back in his chair. "No, we wouldn't expect you to do that."

Ludwig continued. "Getting back to Parnelli, how does he act? In self-interest. Not a crime. Psychology, as well as theology, excuse me for stepping on your toes, tells us, and so does economics, that most of us most of the time act out of self-interest. And your mother tells me from her half-hour interaction with the guy not too long ago, that even when he talks religion, he's still wrapped up in his own person. What is his motive? I don't know, but I can tell you that intention and motive are two of the hardest items to prove in court."

"You don't believe his religious motive for wanting to meet us?" Jeremy asked.

"Let's say I'm skeptical. And excuse me for playing the devil's advocate, so to speak, reverend, but I think the only image he truly worships is the one he sees in the mirror. This is one of the weirdest cases I've ever seen. It's irrational, to the point of being bizarre. We came up with a way for him to hand over some medical papers, absolve him of any financial or other obligations, promise never to bother him again. Instead, he jeopardizes his personal finances and business interests, all in order to do the right thing, follow his conscience. You tell me, reverend, how would you read this?"

"Well, if he's been saved, then maybe he is trying to get right with God and with his fellow man."

"Could be. Could be. You're the expert here. I don't have any direct line to God. But I can tell you flat out, he managed to get his own lawyer...," and he bit his tongue, "ticked off with him, and he sure isn't square with me. His antics have cost us all a lot of trouble and loss of sleep. If this is his way of getting right with his fellow man, then I'm going to win next year's Nobel prize for peace."

A little levity helped the situation, laughter breaking the tension.

"Folks, we can talk this to death. But what I'm hearing is a meeting, with all possible precautions and safeguards. Faith and Scott, you haven't weighed in on this. Are you aboard?"

Faith and Scott nodded, followed by Scott's confirmation. "Whatever the guys decide, we're with them."

Jon added, "Of course we want to keep this private, that's one reason for not going to court. No names, addresses, identities."

Bill said, "I'm glad you mentioned that. I assumed that, but it's good we all understand it in advance. And if you all are agreed on this, I'll call Simon and get the ball rolling. He'll have to get back to his client, so let's get some potential dates, Jeremy."

CHAPTER 33

"Stanley, Bill Ludwig. How are things in Peoria?"

"Fine. You?"

"Okay. Listen, Stan, I've got something for you and your client. My people don't like a meeting at all. But just to get rid of the whole affair, they're willing to discuss a meeting, if we can have it on our terms. Very reasonable."

"Shoot."

"Okay. This time no monkey shit. You know, last time we got burned because Parnelli didn't deliver the goods. Then he tried to prevent Faith from leaving. So first of all, we want the records verified and deposited with a third party. Next, the meeting's got to be in my offices. Turf we can make sure is safe for our client, not the open space of a restaurant. And a half hour. You have to be present to corral and rein in your client. We have the child and myself. Those are the terms we're willing to offer. But not negotiate. So if crazy cowboy Parnelli wants to dick around with the conditions, tell him the deal is off. We're not going to make any idle threats. But if he holds out on the records, even after we've offered a meeting, which we don't have to, then we'll figure not only is he a blackmailer, he's a stupid blackmailer."

"Bill, those terms seem reasonable to me, and I'll do everything I can to get him to accept them. You know how stubborn and emotional he is. Well, he used to be more flexible, but after he went through his religious change, he's trying to put his heart ahead of both his head and his shorts."

"Stan, I don't need to remind you, it's in your best interests to persuade him...well, force him, whatever, to accept this deal. And remember, one reason we're willing to put up with this nonsense is to get the speedy delivery of the records. So this week we seal the deal, next week we consummate it. Otherwise, it's off."

"I understand."

"Stanley?"

"Yes."

"Please don't disappoint me."

∼

"DOUG, IT'S STAN."

"Yeah, legal beagle. What's up?"

"We have a deal with Chicago for a meeting."

"See. What'd I tell you? Us downstate rats can negotiate with those Chicago cats."

"Don't get so smug, Doug. If this deal doesn't come off right, we're both in big trouble."

"What can go wrong?"

"Well, for starters, you need to hand over the records to me, and they get checked and held by a third party."

"Like Hell! That's my trump card. You don't think I'm stupid enough to give up the only advantage I have against you two, do you?"

"Like hell you won't! You really are stupid! He has both of us dead to rights on blackmail, and you want to push his buttons. If you're going to be impossible, then I'll butt out and you can butt in. I'll take my chances with the ethics commission, telling them the truth, that you lied to me that you had the papers, and I was only the messenger of your lie, because I never had the papers to see if they were complete."

"Stan, old buddy, you wouldn't do that to me, would you?"

"I'd have to Doug. Your business may be lousy, but suppose somebody pulled your contractor's license? That's what Ludwig is hanging over my head. I could be reprimanded, one step toward disbarment. Now if you screw around with this, suppose your contractor's license was suspended. Would you change your mind?"

"This has nothing to do with my business!"

"Tell that to the people who license you if you're convicted of blackmail."

"Okay, okay, I'll hand over the papers. But don't threaten me."

"You're the one who's threatening. Saying you won't hand over the papers unless you get a meeting."

"We're talking promise, not threat."

"You think so? Figure again. You can be sure of one thing. Ludwig will get the papers or your ass."

"Well, I've got a business to run, so give me the rest of it."

"A half hour in Ludwig's law offices with your child. Ludwig and I have to be present."

"Shit! A lousy half hour is all I get, after a two hour plus trip to Chicago!"

"Take it or leave it. Ludwig said this is the meeting package. Take it all or reject it."

"Or what? Or else?"

"He didn't make any threats. But he knows he has us, you, nailed for blackmail. So he'd probably push the criminal charge first, then the civil proceedings for breach of agreement."

"Huh! And he expects an answer just like that!"

"You're Goddamn right. He wants an answer this week and a meeting next week. If you want to string this out, then he said he might as well spend his time pushing it through the courts."

"Well, my time is valuable, too. Go ahead and tell them we'll accept it."

"No, Doug, I won't. Last time you burned me, got me tied up

with your non-performance and blackmail by making the mistake of believing you when you said you had the papers. I can call him and tell him you accept the deal, but we don't set a time until you show me the papers and I overnight them to a third party in Chicago."

"And I thought you were my buddy."

"No, Doug, when it's a crime, like blackmail, it's called a conspirator. A co-conspirator. But that I do not intend to be or become. So bring or send the papers over today."

"You're a hardass, Stan."

"Not yet, Doug, but if I keep dealing with you, I'll learn to become one."

~

"BILL, IT'S STAN."

"Good morning, Stan, always good talking to you. Good news today?"

"Yes. Parnelli agreed to the terms."

"And the papers?"

"Yeah, like you said, I told him he had to give them to me. He didn't like it, so I had to play hardball with him, and he's delivered them."

"Are they complete?"

"As far as I can tell. The medical records of three siblings of his parents. Those are the only brothers/sisters he told me about. So it looks like they're complete."

"You can relay to him if they're not, we're coming after him. He runs a contracting business, right?"

"Yes."

"Well, tell him the Better Business Bureau, the contractor's association, the licensing bureau, they'll all be notified if we get burned this time."

"I don't think that's necessary."

"Well, it might be good for you to make sure it's not necessary. I don't have any intentions of visiting this scene again. If Parnelli thinks we're playing cat and mouse, just let him know that we've got a trap big enough for whatever species of rodent he is."

"I'll tell him that."

"Good."

They set the time for the next Thursday at two in Ludwig's office.

"Doug, it's Stan again. And we have a meeting. While we were setting it up, he told me to make sure that you have all the records of all your parents' siblings. If you don't, he'll be notifying the Better Business Bureau, the contracting association, and the contractors' license bureau."

"Wow. Is he a hotshot lawyer or a mafia goon?"

"What about it, Doug? Remember, you didn't tell anyone about your paternity suit, and it came back to haunt you. Are there any other skeletons in the family closet?"

"No, dipstick. And tell your lawyer friend in Chicago that his mother barks at the moon."

"Doug, you'd better settle down before we get to Chicago. You can blow off to me, but if you get nasty with him, he'll throw you out of his office."

"Hah! Him and who else?"

"Him and his building security. And the Chicago Police Department. Any other questions?"

CHAPTER 34

*A*s soon as Parnelli agreed to Ludwig's terms, Faith called Father Whitmore and made an appointment. She felt better as soon as she entered his office.

"Yes, Father, you don't need to ask, I'm in trouble. Well, it's not me so much as my son Jeremy. Doug won't give us the rest of the records unless he has a meeting with his child."

"What for?"

"I've told you, he's born again, and trying to do the right thing, or that's what he says, but it seems to me just another egomaniacal ploy."

"If he wanted to help Jeremy, he'd just overnight the records."

"Yeah, instead of keeping us waiting, dangling."

He asked, "So what do you want to talk about? I mean, you've already cleared all this with your lawyer, right?"

"Yes, so there's no point rehashing it with him. But there's one part of this that bugs me. When Jeremy and Jon discussed the question of whether Jeremy should meet Doug, they got into a big disagreement. Jeremy argues that even if Doug has done bad things, been a sinner, and so on, the fact that he claims to be saved means we should help him improve his life. Meet him and I don't know what all."

"Faith, we talked about that before, and we know that all people are sinners. All people need help. Now whether you need to help him in this way at this time is another matter. So what is it you're driving at?"

"I'm afraid if Jeremy gets involved with Doug, and tries to help...reform him...gosh, I don't know what all, then he'll bring him into the family, and Doug will just ruin our family harmony. He's taking a risk meeting Doug, and the contact with Doug may spill over to the rest of us."

"I see what you're saying, and you're right. Once you get involved with him, it'd be complicated and sticky...to get uninvolved."

"You see that, Scott and I see it, and so does Jon. But Jeremy, to be frank, is in the same born-again dimension of Christianity, and I'm afraid he'll let his soft-hearted do-good mentality lead him into a real soft-headed do-bad act."

"What can you do?"

"Yes, Father, that's the question I brought with me today. What can I do?"

"Gee, I guess that question backfired on me. I don't have any answer."

"Well, I'm not going to sit here and whine and take up your time. I have just two requests for you. The first is to pray for me. The second is to ask for an update on the stained glass window."

"I'll be glad to pray for you. Have been right along. And the building committee was glad to receive your request. Like you wanted, I kept it confidential, but they made me agree to give you their hearty thanks. Anyway, what you wanted, well, we've got windows featuring Jesus, the Bible, the disciples, so one of Mary and child would balance real well. The cost is considerable, easily ten-fifteen thousand."

"How about if I get my bank to deposit in the church's account that amount, say fifteen thousand?"

"You'd go that much?"

"Yes. My health insurance won't cover it, but I figure you've saved me and my insurance company about that amount in shrinkage fees."

"Shrinkage?"

"Shrink fees."

"Clever, Faith. I'll email you the account numbers, and the only thing anyone will know is an account number. You still want it anonymous?"

"Yes. My reward will be seeing the window when I attend church."

CHAPTER 35

*R*achel and Jon had not talked about the rendezvous Jeremy was scheduled to have with Doug. When they learned the actual day and time, she waited until the kids were in bed, then she asked Jon to take a break from his internet surfing and sit at the kitchen table with her.

"Jon, have you thought any more about Jeremy going face to face with...your father?"

"Babe, can't get it out of my mind."

"And what do you think about it?"

"All kinds of things. Still have reservations about it. Then I figure he and the lawyer can handle it. Because the protection is in place. Kind of like anti-virus software. Then again, I know there's always a new virus popping up. And what scares the holy Bejesus out of me is that our father, and I use that word loosely, seems to be a worse worm than any software virus. That makes me afraid of what trouble he might cause for all of us."

"Jon, is that all you think?"

"What do you mean?"

"Did you ever think of stopping Jeremy from meeting him?"

"Rachel! You know I couldn't do that! The time and place are set, and to back out now would wreck our chance of getting the records."

"The meeting has to go forward?"

"Sure. I don't see any other way. Do you?"

"No other way? Jeremy has to get together with this...Doug?"

"He can't hardly back out now."

She corrected him. "Can't hardly?"

"Uh...what?"

"Can hardly."

"Okay, Miss spell/grammar checker, can hardly."

"Yes, Jon. He can hardly back out. How do you feel about that?"

"Well, I don't like it, but you know I can't do anything about it now."

"You can't?"

"No, Rachel. I can't stop it."

"You're right. You can't stop it. But can you help it?"

"Rachel! Are you suggesting what I believe you are?"

"Let me put it to you this way. How would you feel if you had to go toe to toe with Doug? You'd have this fancy lawyer with you, yes, but would you appreciate having anyone else with you?"

"God! Are you the devil's advocate or the angels' auxiliary?"

"You see what I mean?"

"Yes. And you're very clever, slipping me into his shoes and having me look at Doug through Jeremy's eyes. Yes. Of course. I'd much rather have him with me."

"You would?"

"Sure, Rachel. But the meeting and conditions are set, so now we can't change it."

"You mean you'd be willing to go with Jeremy if that was the agreement?"

"Yeah, I guess so. But," he sputtered, "Rachel, the deal is set. It can't be changed! Not now!"

"Well, you know the agreement was for Doug to meet his child."

"Yes."

"And aren't you his child?"

"Sure! You're right! Jeremy's his child. I'm his child. So each of us would be fulfilling the terms of the agreement."

"I'm not a lawyer, but it sounds kosher to me."

"If you're not a lawyer, you sure have the mind for it. Kosher! Legal. Legit. Hey, that's good! Okay, Miss regal eagle with the fancy legal wiggle, since you got me into this, do you think Jeremy would even let me tag along?"

"I'm sure he would. But I'm not the one to ask. If you want to know, why don't you ask him?"

"Well, Rachel, you could have saved us twenty minutes if you'd just have said, Jon, pick up the phone and call Jeremy, tell him you're going with him to the meeting."

"If I came right out and told you, you wouldn't do it. You had to see it yourself."

"Yeah. But I didn't see it myself. You saw it myself."

Rachel kissed him.

"Hi, Jeremy, it's your brother. The one who lives in Oak Park."

"Hi, Jon. Mom told you about the agreement, didn't she?"

"Yeah. She called us. Matter of fact, Rachel and I were just talking about it, and I wondered...well, actually it was Rachel's idea, but I think it's a good idea if you could go along with it if...I went along with you to the meeting."

Jeremy didn't say anything.

"Jeremy?"

"Yes."

"I mean, if it's okay with you. If not, I'll understand."

"No, no, Jon. I think it's a great idea. It's just that you took me by surprise. You haven't changed your mind about the meeting, have you?"

"No. I still think it's a risky business. In fact, I guess that's why Rachel and I figured it's a good idea for me to go with you. We could back each other up."

"Well, let's see, we'd have to clear this with Ludwig, wouldn't we? I don't know if he'd agree to that. It's not what we talked about."

"Yes, but listen to what Rachel figured out. The agreement was for our father to see his child, and you're his child, and I'm his child, so each of us fulfills the terms of the agreement."

"Wow! If I ever need a lawyer, I'll contact Rachel."

"You'll have to stand in line after me, because she handles my legal paper first."

"Jon, I feel much better knowing you'll be there with me. It was good just to hear you say you wanted to be there."

"Well, after all, Jeremy, you know what the Good Book says, don't you?"

"What?"

"Am I my brother's keeper?"

It took Jeremy a while to respond. "Yes, Jon...you are my keeper, and I appreciate it."

Melanie could tell from one half of the conversation the gist of the call. And she could see from the tears on Jeremy's face what it meant to him.

"HELLO, Bill, this is Jon Rockwell, Faith Armstrong's son. The one from Oak Park. Thanks for taking my call. I know you're very busy."

"Yes, Jon, I remember you well from the meeting in my office with your brother Jeremy. And you told the receptionist this is about the meeting? I have to ask you to give it to me quickly, because I've only got a few minutes. A client is waiting."

"Sure. I won't go into all the reasons, but I'd like to be with Jeremy when he meets our father."

"You would? Well...why?"

"He and I have gone through a lot in the past couple of years, and even though we don't agree completely on this meeting, I think it's my responsibility to be with him. After all, we're twins, and we've got to pull together."

"That's a heavy responsibility."

"It's not heavy, it's my brother."

Bill Ludwig didn't have time for humor. "Jon, the only catch is that's not in the agreement."

Jon told Ludwig how Rachel had seen through Jeremy's solo agreement, taking the "child" clause literally and turning it into a "twofer" twin deal without actually violating the terms of the arrangement.

Ludwig had to agree. "Jesus, Joseph, and Mary! Scott's a research-detective whiz, your mother's a bang-up negotiator, and you and your spouse are legal casuists."

"Legal what?"

"Casuists. In the middle ages in the church, the theologians who could twist a phrase inside out, make it mean anything they wanted it to."

"Uh, is that good or bad?"

"Jon, when it works for us, it's good. Very good. Now I've got to get to my client. See you in my office at 1:30 Thursday."

"I'll be there."

"And Jon, you know, I'm beginning to look forward to this meeting. Think it will be fun. Your father has given us a double dose of doo-doo, and now we'll return the favor with a double dip of our own."

CHAPTER 36

*J*eremy came with his family the day before the meeting, staying with Jon. Scott and Faith made a mid-week sojourn to the burbs for the occasion.

Time was short, so Scott had planned ahead. He checked with Melanie and Rachel, asking if they'd used the canvas glove puppet idea. Both sheepishly admitted they had not gotten around to it. He was glad, because he brought along a whole box of the gloves, and had made his own glove-puppet, as well as one for each of the kids, using different colors for each of the five finger-faces on a glove.

When the children tackled him, wanting to know what they were going to do, he was carrying the box of gloves, wrapped and decorated with a big bow. And they knew he was up to something. "I just happened to bring some of my friends along, and they'd like to play with you. They're very handy. I have to hand it to them. Well, maybe I can hand this box to you, and maybe you can give them a hand if they give you a hand." Jeb was the designated box-opener, and they couldn't wait for him to open it. When he managed to get the paper off, they were delighted.

Scott held his hands out in front of him using his forefinger and thumb to form a digital pistol. "I'm the gangsta! Hands up, everyone!"

As the kids held their hands above their heads, Scott outfitted everyone with a pair of cotton gloves. Then he donned his own pre-painted pair, featuring ten mini-faces, one for each finger. "Okay, kids, I've handed 'em to you, now you've got to face your own gloves."

The kids didn't need to get the puns to catch on to the game.

Tipped off ahead of time, Rachel had the puppet theater's cardboard stage and the markers ready. Each child made a hand puppet. Then they were off and play-acting.

While the kids were busy, Faith took Jeremy aside. "Jeremy, I don't often ask you to do something, but I'm asking now. It's a mother's prerogative to protect her children. What I'm asking you to do is for your own good. I don't think you'll like it, but please do it as a favor for me."

"Mom, what is it you can ask me that you think I won't do?"

She pulled out of her purse her small mini-recorder, that looked like a pen. "Wear this when you have the meeting and turn it on. It will record your meeting. And then if we ever need to use it against your father, we'll have it."

"Mother...that's not in the agreement...to have a recording."

"No. It's not. And it's not in the agreement not to have a recording."

"Do you think Ludwig would okay it?"

"Ludwig wouldn't, won't, can't. It would be unethical for him to record an attorney and client without their permission."

"What about me?"

"You're doing a favor for me. If it ever came up, you could say I asked you to. For your own protection. Because he half threatened me, almost physically detained me, I was afraid for you, and asked you to take this along for your own good. Hey, I'm not snoopy. If after the meeting you don't want me to hear it, that's fine. But if he does get out of line, you'll have a record of his bad behavior."

"Well, if you really want me to...yes, I'll do it."

"Good. Let's keep this between you and me. I don't think Jon should know about this. I mean, I don't want him staring at it."

"No."

She showed him how to turn it on. "It has fresh batteries in it, and will record for ninety minutes."

~

JON SAID, "Jeremy! It's time for us to take off."

As they drove from Oak Park in to the Loop for the meeting, Jeremy said, "Jon, remember when we went to Canton to the adoption agency?"

"Can't forget it."

"I was nervous as a wet hen."

Jon chuckled.

"And you were this cool cucumber, just saying you'd play it by ear, and to trust you and go along with you."

"Pretty cocky, huh?"

"Confident."

"And?"

"Jon, I want to put two things in the record before we have this meeting. One is I can't tell you how important it is to me that you decided to come with me and support me. The other is, no matter what happens in the meeting, we're in this together, and we'll get through it. You asked me to trust you in Canton, so I'm asking you to trust me now."

"Sure thing, bro."

CHAPTER 37

They were in Ludwig's office at one thirty. He ushered them into the conference room so the twins wouldn't bump into Doug and Simon when they appeared. A few minutes later he joined them.

"Well, boys, are we ready for our meeting?"

Jeremy looked around the room. "I thought I'd be ready, but actually I'm kind of nervous."

Ludwig nodded. "And rightly so. If you weren't a little anxious, you wouldn't be prepared to deal with a difficult situation. And you know that the time until we bring in Simon and Parnelli, I'm just going to chit-chat with you and give you a chance to ask last minute questions. Put you at ease. In the trade, we call this the hand-holding session. But before we get to that, or part of it, Jeremy, my manners weren't very good the last time. I didn't even ask about your medical condition. How's it going?"

"Much better. My kidney function has improved, above fifty percent. And they're not sure why, but one reason for the additional records is to make sure there's no hereditary kidney failure on my father's side."

"That's great. You know, since my attack, I've had a significant change of outlook. Doctors do people a lot of good. When I reflect on my lawyering, most of the work I've done is penny-ante, saving rich people tax bucks, handling divorces and custody disputes, you know, most of it squabbles, quibbles. But doctors come through in life-saving situations. And when I look at you two, and your mother and Scott, you're the salt of the earth. Your father, I must say, is the scum of the earth. So doing the right thing here, helping you keep your family together, is one of the best things I can do. Well, end of sermon. We've got a few minutes, and I should let you ask any final questions."

Jon said, "Why don't you just give us advice on how to handle the situation."

"My first piece of advice is to watch out for Mr. Parnelli. He's smart, clever, charming. He's a con man, and he'll try to con you. Get you on his side. Whine, wheedle, whimper, get you to feeling sorry for him. My advice is don't go sentimental and buy his con."

Jon asked, "How can we do that?"

"Well, your mother taped the meeting she had with him, and I heard it. She had the best strategy I can recommend to you. Let him talk. Give him a yes or no or simple answer. You don't have to ask him any questions. He's so self-absorbed, he's ink and blotter all in one. Just let him rattle on for a half hour, then we have the ticket for the third party to give us the records."

Jeremy shrugged. "You're only concerned with the records."

"Yes! That's what this meeting is about. Well, two things. One, getting the records. Two, getting the records without any harm done to your family."

Jeremy asked, "You're not concerned with our father's well-being?"

"No. Not in the slightest. Jeremy, pardon me my lawyer's tunnel vision, but for your own good, I'm single-minded: serving my clients. I was hired to get these documents, as quickly and safely as possible. I can't afford to worry about the other guy."

"I guess that goes against the grain for me. I think we should be concerned for others."

"That's why Simon is here. He'll take care of Parnelli. We take care of us. I'm not a priest. I don't grant absolution. I'm not a psychiatrist. I don't administer therapy. I'm a lawyer. I advise and litigate. For my clients. If I was concerned for the other client, you should find another lawyer who will work for you. And right now I'm advising you to keep us and our goal as your first and only concern."

Jeremy looked down. "It won't be easy."

"No, these things are never easy. But we get through them. We do that by keeping in mind what our goal is, and by hanging together."

Jon wondered, "How will you handle the meeting?"

"I'll bring in Simon and Parnelli, introduce you two. First names only! For the meeting let's use 'Jeremy' and 'Jonathan.' I'll just assume that the two of you being here is naturally what we expected all along. I'll remind them they have a half hour, and point out the time. Then as much as possible, we'll let Parnelli run his mouth. Please, please keep your answers simple. And don't get sucked into his con. Now if I see you rambling on, or if Parnelli gets too probing, I'll step in and change the subject."

At ten to two the receptionist stuck her head in the conference room. "Mr. Simon and Mr. Parnelli are here for their two o'clock."

"Fine. Tell them we'll be with them shortly."

Jeremy said, "Well, I guess we don't have any more questions. Right Jon?" He nodded. "So you can begin any time you want to."

"Jeremy, they've kept us waiting all this time. So now it's our turn to have them wait. We don't want to appear to be over-eager for this meeting."

They talked until a few minutes past two. "Well, that's long enough. I'll go get them."

Jeremy looked nervously at Jon, and fumbled with his pen.

"Jeremy, you don't need a pen, do you? What's there to take notes on? And anyway, we have legal pads and pencils."

Ludwig returned a few minutes later. He had seated Jeremy and Jon next to each other on one side of a long conference table, and had pulled out two chairs opposite the twins, first leading Simon and Parnelli to these two seats, then walking around to sit next to Jeremy. As he moved around the table, slowly and calmly, he announced deliberately, "The meeting is now convened. Please note that the wall clock gives the time as five minutes past two. At thirty-five minutes past the hour the meeting is closed."

Simon and Parnelli, however, did not even glance at the clock. Their eyes were fixed on the twin images before them.

"This is Mr. Simon, this is Mr. Parnelli. And here are Jeremy and Jonathan, the offspring of your union with Faith."

Simon's jaw was agape. Doug turned with a look of surprise toward Simon, and then a flash of anger toward Ludwig. "You said... 'my child'...I thought...."

Ludwig said, "That's right. Your child Jeremy has a medical problem. And your child Jonathan may have the same problem later. These things tend to run in families, and that's why we've been trying these past months to get the medical records, so the doctors can rule out a hereditary factor and pin down the diagnosis."

Doug said, "But I didn't know...twins!"

Ludwig added, "Yes, identical twins."

Doug snapped, "Yes, I can see that. If I'd only known, I'd have...."

Jon blurted out, "You'd have what? Married our mother?"

Doug said, "Well, I'd have done the right thing."

Jeremy demanded, "What would the right thing have been?"

"Well, I'd have taken care of you...and your mother."

Ludwig was following the flow of the conversation, and let the interchange continue.

Jon said, "Well, nothing stopped you."

Doug hesitated. "Your mother...never told me. She—"

Jon cut in. "And you never asked."

Ludwig felt it was time to step in. "Jonathan and Jeremy, we agreed to this half hour with Mr. Parnelli, and it's his time, so maybe he'd like to do the talking."

Doug began. "Yeah. I do. It's just that...I never expected this. Twins. Identical twins. And, well, I guess you people know all about me, I've got other kids. But none of them resemble me like you two do. Spittin' image. You two look almost exactly like I did when I was your age. So I can't get over it. Now I forget what I was going to say when I got here.

"Well, yeah, let me try to begin where I started with your mother. Guess I didn't do a very good job with her. Apologizing. I tried to tell her I'm sorry for not knowing about you, not doing anything for you all these years. Maybe it's too late now to do anything, but I just wanted to let you know that I'm sorry. And I hope you can forgive me for making life...difficult for you and your mother."

He waited for them to speak. Jeremy looked toward Jon, who only clenched his jaw in silence, moving his head ever so slightly in a negative gesture.

"Well, I can't blame you two for not falling all over yourselves to welcome me with open arms. I suppose your mother has told you all kinds of bad things about me. And...," he turned and glared at Ludwig, "this...lawyer probably didn't say anything nice about me, either."

Ludwig was the perfect angel, not the least perturbed by the innuendo, which he neither confirmed nor denied, his gaze directed at the opposite wall.

Doug turned toward Jeremy and Jon. "Well, he won't say anything now. That's alright. Like he said, it's my time. And not much of it. So I have to tell you what I can and show you I'm not the rotten tomato your mother and this lawyer have made me out to be.

"I can't deny, a lot of the things you've heard about me are true. Sure, I've been the ladies' man. I was attracted to girls, and they were attracted to me. So I'm only human. Maybe I shouldn't have been with so many, but that's the past. What can I do about that? Nothing. I can only deal with the present. And the future.

"You know I was married twice. And have kids by both wives. And another by a woman who lived with me. I—"

Jon blurted out, "How many—?"

Ludwig reached in front of Jeremy and placed his hand on Jon's. "Let him finish."

"Yeah. Let me finish. I ain't got much time. Sure, you know about that old paternity suit. I already admitted I was a bad actor. Behaved badly. But I was young at the time...."

Jon leaned forward, ready to contradict this last statement, but Ludwig turned toward him and signaled with a negative shake of his head. Jon settled back in his chair.

"Uh-huh. I've screwed up real bad. My wives remarried, took my houses, turned my children against me. I'm pretty much alone. And I got to thinking about myself. And I didn't like too much what I saw. When I got to talking with some of the guys at my construction company, you know, they're a pretty rough crew, construction workers, well, some of them had led wild lives, like me, and they turned over a new leaf, changed. So I went with them to some meetings, got saved, and now I'm trying to turn my life around, make things right with the people I wronged, make things up."

Now Jeremy moved forward, about to chime in. Ludwig casually rested his hand on Jeremy's shoulder, smiling at him. Jeremy sighed and leaned back.

Doug didn't notice the move, wrapped up in his own story. "I never went to church much, but these revival people are different. They take you where you are, and turn you around. They show you where you've been, what you've done wrong, and how you can remodel your life. You've gone your own selfish way. Well, that's what I've been telling you about, all my mistakes. I was always living life my way. But they showed me there's only one way to lead your life, God's way."

At the words "one way," Jeremy sat up straight in his chair, eyes wide in amazement, and opened his mouth to speak, just as Jon kicked him. Jeremy flinched, and gave Jon a hurt look. Doug was oblivious to the brotherly exchange.

"The One Way people show you that you have to give up your

worldly ways, selfish ways, and take on Christ's way, God's way. That's what 'One Way' means, short for One Way for God."

Jon glared at Jeremy, who was squirming in his chair.

"Well, my time is short for today. And I probably can't persuade you to change your minds about me in just thirty minutes. I tried to get your mother to agree to more time, and let me get to know you. She wouldn't even hear of it. That's why I gave up on her, and figured I could talk to you directly. And even if I don't make friends with you today, at least I can tell you about One Way, what changed me for good, turned my life around. If you haven't heard about it, I hope you look them up and go to their meetings."

When Doug got no reply, he plunged ahead. "And if you're busy, you don't even have to go to their meetings. They've even got a One Way handheld to take with you." From his pocket he pulled out an electronic DigiOneway.

This time it was Jon's jaw that came unlocked and fell open in surprise. And Jeremy found his opportunity to return the favor of a kick in the shins. Jon jerked. As Jon turned toward Jeremy he detected a slight smirk on his brother's face.

Ludwig was biding his time, as the hands of the wall clock moved toward the half-hour point punctuating the end of the meeting.

Doug said, "This little thing, battery powered, you can take with you, in the car, to work, on a trip, and you can mark your daily devotions, and also your progress as you get rid of selfish ways and move toward the true One Way."

Now Jon was uncomfortable, unable to sit still. He looked anxiously at the clock, which finally advanced from two thirty to two thirty-five. Doug glanced at the clock, and was speeding up, trying to get some last remarks in.

"I hope you two can forgive me. I'm trying to change, and hope you'll help me. I can't undo what I've done in the past, but I'm starting now. I know the agreement was only for this half hour, and the lawyer's going to kick me out pretty quick. But I'm giving you my card, and hope that you'll contact me and let me meet with you again. If you could...would...give me your name and...."

Ludwig stepped in as referee again. "Yes, Mr. Parnelli, as you said, the time is over, and it is my duty to end this meeting. Now if you and Mr. Simon would kindly depart my office."

Doug didn't get up from his chair. With a wild-eyed look, he begged, "Can you forgive me?"

Jeremy mumbled, "I...forgive you." He turned to Jon, and asked, "For me...?"

Jon didn't say anything, just nodded his head up and down.

"Great. It was worth this meeting, to see you both. And to receive your forgiveness."

Ludwig had walked around the table, and said firmly. "Mr. Parnelli, the meeting is over."

"No, the meeting has just begun. I've been reunited with my sons."

Simon had said nothing the entire meeting. Now Ludwig spoke loudly and authoritatively. "Mr. Simon, will you please see that your client abides by our agreement, and leaves. Otherwise...."

Simon stood up, took his client by the arm, and said, "Doug, come on. It's over."

"Not yet. I'm not done here."

Ludwig stepped back around the table, and motioned the twins to follow him. Jon got up quickly, and had to perform an arm-pull on Jeremy to get him to move. Ludwig circled behind them, placed his hands in the small of each twin's back, and herded them toward the back door of the conference room, as Doug raised his voice, "Wait, don't go," and tried to follow them, restrained by Simon.

Ludwig stepped back into the conference room, not the least bit agitated. "Gentlemen, our meeting is over. We have need of this room in a few minutes, so please be good enough to vacate it. Otherwise, security will clear it."

Doug's face flushed, as he cried openly. He started to lunge toward Ludwig. Simon stepped in between them. Ludwig didn't budge.

"Very well. As you wish. Security will be here in a few minutes."

Simon spoke up. "Bill, that won't be necessary. We're leaving."

"I'm concerned for my own safety and the safety of my clients. I'm going into my office and making the call."

CHAPTER 38

*J*on and Jeremy talked non-stop after the meeting. Ludwig had another client, so after listening to the two of them for a few minutes, he ended it with, "You boys did good. Your mama should be proud of you. It was tough, but we got through it. And now the third party will deliver us the records. Once Simon gives them the green light, they should hand them over. Probably tomorrow. I'll call Faith when they're here."

Jeremy was upset. "And then what?"

Ludwig raised his eyebrows. "You're on an adrenalin rush now. I'm used to these meetings. As used to them as I'll ever get. Don't do a single thing now. Give it a few days to cool before you even start to consider all this. Have one of your famous family get-togethers. The best bit of advice I can give you now is to maintain your family unity. It's the best thing you've got going for you. And I don't include that Peoria...I was going to say perp, but will keep it polite, that Peoria person in the family."

Jon and Jeremy headed for the door.

"Oh, one more thing. The receptionist will show you the way to a service elevator. It gets you out of the building from a back entrance. An alley way. Not too pretty, but if Parnelli gets cute and tries to waylay you, waiting at the front entrance, he'll be sorely disappointed. Don't want you to have to handle him on your own."

The twins talked as they walked on the way to pick up the car in a parking lot and kept it up as they returned to Oak Park.

Jon lashed out, "I hate that man."

"Jon, hate is a strong word."

"Is it stronger than detest?"

"You don't mean that, surely."

"Sorry, Jeremy, know it goes against your religion, but he's a thousand per cent self-centered."

"Can't disagree with you there."

"Bill let him talk, and mostly it was about poor me. My sad life. Pity me. Forgive me."

"Well, Jon, I do appreciate the fact that you did signal your forgiveness of him."

"It's the least I could do. For you, Jeremy, not for him."

"He's the one who needs the forgiveness."

"He needs more than that, a total rebuild, a reconstruction job from the ground up."

"Yes, Jon, he's trying to make things right, he says."

"But Jeremy, during his precious half hour not once did he ask about your medical condition, or how the records might affect our whole family."

"You're absolutely right. That's what I noticed. It's what he didn't say that surprised me."

"Well, Jeremy, I know your religion is important to you, but he's hiding behind his religion. And what he's hiding is his selfish, self-centered, egotistical, macho...I don't know what."

"Yes. I can't disagree there."

Jon frowned. "He uses One Way, and DigiOneway, both, as shields to prevent himself and others from seeing his ugly selfishness."

"Yes, he does."

"I wanted to grab that DigiOneway and take it away from him."

"You're right, Jon. I wanted to tell him that he doesn't understand One Way. He mouths the words, but he doesn't act it out in his life."

When they reached Oak Park, Jeremy and Melanie had to get the kids in the car quickly to beat the rush out of Chicago. Jeremy and Jon agreed they would talk later. Jon told Rachel he'd fill her in but needed to call his mother first. Rachel picked up from what she overheard, that Ludwig had already called Faith, and Jon ended the conversation quickly, saying things had gone well, and they would have the records in a day or two. He gave Rachel a quick summary of the meeting.

Jon was upset. "I wish I'd never developed DigiOneway, if nuts like Doug could use it the way he did."

"Jon, remember, it's just a tool. A hammer is a tool. It's intended for building houses. It's good. But someone can pick up a hammer and kill with it. That doesn't make the hammer bad. The person who uses a hammer for the wrong purpose is bad. A knife can be used to cut food, or to stab a person. So don't blame the tool for what the person using it does with it. It's the same with DigiOneway."

"I know you're right, but I'm still mad at that...well, to use the lawyer's term, perp."

CHAPTER 39

Shortly after Jeremy and Melanie hit the road, the children were asleep, so they could talk freely. Jeremy replayed the meeting as quickly as he could.

"Jeremy, it does sound like everyone's fear of your father has some basis. He seems to be a real loser. What do you think?"

"I know he's a loser. But Melanie, losers need help, love, too. What you and I have always said is that losers, sinners, need help more than the winners, the saints."

"What do you intend to do?"

"I don't know. Our father wants to maintain contact with us. Jon doesn't like that at all. But I don't know how to refuse him."

"Jeremy, think that over for a minute. You're on the outs with your adoptive parents because of your split from the Lutheran church. And you've never had a relationship with this...Doug. He's been too busy chasing women all over Illinois."

"He never knew mom was pregnant."

"Jeremy! He was there when it happened! So he could have come back and found out if his fun had any consequences. I can't give him any excuse there."

"No, Melanie, I guess I can't either."

"Well, let's not argue about that. But look at it this way. Scott is the one who actually put this family together. He located and identified you two, then helped you find your mother. And I've never seen a more dedicated Grandpa than him. I don't know what you intend to do, but you've got a long way to go to convince me to let Mark and Beth call him Grandpa. He doesn't deserve it. Scott does, and it would be unfair to take that away from him."

Jeremy thought they were done with the conversation, when Melanie changed the subject. "You know, Jeremy, it's been more than a year since you took over the Mothers and Children Fund, and it's time you thought about the future. What you want to do. Where we're going. What do you think?"

"You know, Melanie, that's been on my mind, too. The foundation can make a big difference for a lot of people. And I worry that splitting my time between One Way and the foundation isn't fair to either. Let's talk about it."

FAITH PICKED up the medical records, which Ludwig had retrieved from the third party through a messenger service. She overnighted them to Jeremy in Springfield. The doctors confirmed there was no genetic predisposition to kidney failure.

Faith told Scott, "We went through months of Hell just to get a negative finding."

"You're right."

"Well, we met the devil, and so did our twin angels, and we beat Lucifer! But the reward is just an empty prize."

Scott shook his head. "Babe, don't you realize, this is the best possible news. A positive finding would have meant the likelihood of increasingly diminished kidney function, then dialysis, and possibly an organ transplant. And maybe problems for Jon and the grandkids."

She looked him in the eye. "You didn't talk to the doctors."

"No, but I got help from the science editor at the paper, and he helped me research the issue."

"You didn't tell me."

"Didn't want to scare you. But that's what convinced me to go along with the meetings, not wait around."

"Come here, you smart ass dumb fool!" She threw her arms around him and gave him a big kiss.

JON WANTED to follow up on the prayer angle for the next version of Digirel, so Faith had him come along on her next visit to Father Whitmore.

"Jon, I've heard a lot about you, and am pleased to meet you. And to tell the truth, I'm a little nervous about what your mother told me, that my prayer gimmicks might find their way into Digirel."

"Don't worry. I'm the novice here. Just taking tips from the professionals."

Father Whitmore explained again prayer to, through, and for. Jon took notes and said that would be easy to program into Digirel.

Then Father Whitmore showed them the artist's rendition of the stained glass window Faith had commissioned. Faith was pleased, telling Father Whitmore to go ahead and have the window made.

On the way back to the condo, Jon told her that he understood the connection between the Mothers and Children Foundation and the stained glass window. She just smiled.

JON ALWAYS CONSULTED with Dr. Handy before making any adjustments to Digirel. Dr. Handy fully approved of Father Whitmore's prayer plan. And he added two more touches. He said, "In a number of religions, prayer is 'on' something. You know, a physical object, such as a rosary, is the concrete means, or aid, on which prayer depends. Buddhism and Islam, as well as Christianity, use prayer beads. And prayer can be 'at' something. The something can be an abstract virtue, such as love, or it can be visual/mental focus directed at a mandala or other symbolic representation."

The new version of Digirel provided a pull-down menu of prayer

to

through

for

on

at

with a sub-menu for each of these options.

CHAPTER 40

*F*aith returned alone to meet with Father Whitmore.

"Father, you know, when we first started talking, Doug was a question mark. And now he's become a big question again."

"Have you forgiven him?"

"I think so. He's so pathetic I lost my capacity for hating him."

"But he's still a problem?"

"Yes. Not a theological problem, like do I or the twins forgive him. More of a social problem. You know, we have to face whether we'll have any contact with him."

"And you don't want to have anything to do with him?"

"No. The family seems united on that. Except for Jeremy. You know Jeremy, he's got the One Way movement and its manner of looking at things. Everyone is a sinner. Everyone can be saved. Everyone needs help."

"Faith, I know where he's coming from."

"I understand that in theory. But I don't know why we would have to let Doug into our family circle. I think it would be a disaster."

"I think you're right there, Faith."

"You do? Well tell me why I'm right, because I'd sure like to convince Jeremy."

"Well, even if you recognize that everyone's a sinner, it doesn't mean you personally are obligated to see to the salvation of every single human being."

"Sure. That's so obvious I couldn't see it."

"And not being in your family doesn't mean that Doug isn't or can't be saved. You can just direct him to other churches, the One Way movement, whatever."

"The rub is, he asked to be part of the family."

"Faith, you can tell him that because your family has bonded together, he should try to find his social and spiritual peace with his own...family."

"Families."

"Yes, he's been a very busy man."

"Thanks, Father. You never fail to have help for me."

FAITH ALWAYS LOOKED FORWARD to family gatherings at Oak Park. But after the twins' meeting with Doug, things were unsettled. She was uneasy as she and Scott drove out.

Grandpa Scott made his usual circus entrance with the kids, a real four ring extravaganza. By now they knew enough to leave it up to him. He always had a bushel basket of tricks up his sleeve. He didn't even tell Faith what he planned, and she didn't mind. She was like the kids, loved being surprised.

He had each child select their favorite puppet, and act out their best story. While they played puppeteer, he played camera-man, videotaping the performance. Then they had a replay of the video through the television. Stephie summed up the critics' review: "I like the television theater better than the puppet theater."

Faith realized the significance of Scott's performance. He could take a dismal day and make the sun shine on it. He picked up everyone's spirits, especially the adults. They were walking on egg shells, worrying about the family meeting.

After lunch the kids didn't want to go to their video. They wanted to be part of the prayer circle.

Faith felt prayed out. She gave her standard prayer of thanks for the family, petition for guidance and protection.

Rachel had established the ritual batting order, coming up second. She lifted her head up, narrowing her eyes, as if penetrating the skies. "You have given us eyes, Lord, help us to see with them. You have given us ears, Lord, help us to hear with them. You have given us minds, Lord, help us to think with them. You have given us voices, help us to speak with them. You have given us bodies, help us to act with them. We are your servants, help us to obey."

Melanie followed. "Our Father in Heaven, we come to you today as we always do, in time of plenty, in time of want, in time of health, in time of sickness. Today we come together seeking your wisdom. Help us overcome our human foolishness and partake of your divine guidance."

Scott surprised everyone with his own prayer. "Thank you, God, for protecting the children and me while we made our lovely trip on the bus and on the train. We pray for your continued protection in the future."

Beth, who had squeezed between Scott and her father, chimed in one of the few prayers she knew. "God is great, God is good. And we thank him for this food."

Amidst a few stifled adult snickers, Mark stage-whispered, "You're not supposed to pray, silly."

"Am too!"

Jeremy shushed his children, adding his petition. "Oh God, help us today to do the right thing. We pray for your knowledge, your wisdom, your strength."

Jon, the cheese standing alone, was not to be left out. "We pray to the powers above. As we have formed this circle, guide us, and let the perfection of the unbroken circle be our model for our harmony with you and with one another."

Hearty amens followed, and the women shooed the kids into the TV room.

Faith had tipped Scott off that he was to be by her side today, not in kiddie land.

Faith started the discussion. "Folks, we've come a long way these past few months. I'm proud of how you've all worked hard, hung together, shouldered the load. Bill Ludwig said that marriages and families either get stronger or fall apart in times of crisis. I'm glad to see this family rock solid. Yet I also recognize one nagging question, what to do with...about...the twins' father. So the floor is open, and let's hear what's on your minds."

Melanie was next. "Mom, you're right, we've been strong, and we don't want things to fall apart now. But this is a real problem. Even Jeremy and I can't agree on...Doug. Not completely. He'd like to contact his father. I can't blame him. And I understand some of the reasons why. Not just the father-son tie, but in our religious lives we've always tried to help someone, no matter what. This time, I confess, it's different. I don't want my children to have any contact with Doug. He may have his place in Heaven. That's up to God. But he hasn't earned his place in this family. Jeremy, I hate to say this, but we should be honest about it."

Jeremy spoke. "This is a test of faith. Do I like my father? No. Not as a person. But I can't totally reject him as a human being. Every human being is a child of God. So I'm with Melanie on the point that our father hasn't done anything to deserve to be included in this family. However, he can still be a member of the family of God. That's why I can't rule out contacting him."

Jon said, "Jeremy, right after the meeting, I was so mad, I said I hated our father. That was a mistake. And I've learned from mother, and from Father Whitmore, that we can pray to, through, and for. She can tell you more about that. Anyway, I can pray for him. The whole family can pray for him. So not including him in our family circle doesn't mean we've ruled him out of the human race, or excluded him from the family of God."

Rachel looked with pride at her husband, and then glanced at

Melanie. "Let me speak, like Melanie, as a mother. I second Melanie's note about the children. I mean, it's not a simple matter for just one of us to accept Doug, take him in. I can't see him as part of our family. That may be biased, because I haven't met him. But from everything I hear, he's not at all a family man, and at his age I don't think we can change that. If he wants to change, it's up to him. Sure, we can, and should, pray for him. But we have our children to think about. And he's not a child. He should take care of himself."

Jeremy and Jon looked at their mother. She didn't wait for them to have to ask her.

"Well, I speak as a mother and a grandmother. And I'll keep it simple. Melanie and Rachel are right on track. As adults we can handle Doug better. But the children can't. And we're not depriving Doug of his family. He deprived himself of it. He's smart, he's dangerous. I think the less contact with him the better. I follow Jon's suggestion that praying for him is the best way to go."

She looked at Scott.

"Well, people, I'm in an awkward position, having assumed the grandfather's role, the one Doug would have. Or would assume, if he entered the picture. So I've got a vested interest to exclude him. You know how much I appreciate the children. They worship me, and I treasure them. Can I separate my feelings from all this? No! I have selfish interests to protect. But still, I ask you, what can Doug contribute to this family? And I hear myself saying 'nothing.'

"Doug can only detract from the family, weaken it, diminish it, possibly even destroy it. I go along with the others, to pray for him. My dad was a minister, and we prayed for everyone. That's all well and good. But finally, Doug's salvation is an individual matter, between him and God. And his social well-being is something he should work on, that's for sure."

Jeremy was looking down while the others gave their comments. When everyone had spoken, he raised his eyes. "Maybe I'm the lone holdout here. But I listened carefully to your prayers, and what you've said today. And I think you've shown me something I didn't see before. I think we can at least make an indirect contact with

Doug, through Bill Ludwig. We can wish him well, tell him we're praying for him, but say he should find his peace with God, and make peace with his own family, families. I mean the children he lived with. If we do that, I think we can be responsible to God and to...our fellow man."

Everyone nodded their heads to this suggestion, and smiles dissolved the tension they had been feeling, just as Mark and Beth broke into the room. Mark announced, "We're bored." Beth asked, "C'n we do another praying circle? Mark and me didn' get a pray turn."

The adults were glad to oblige them. The children's prayers were more specific with their thanks. Mark prayed, "Dear God, we thank you for Grandpa Scott and the newspaper, the radio broadcast, the television program, and the puppet theater."

Stephie said, "And especially the train."

Beth added. "Yeah, and also the Chicago condo."

The wives took the children to play in a nearby park, allowing Jeremy and Jon to have a little time alone with Faith and Scott. After a few minutes, Jeremy came up with the blockbuster for the day.

"You know, Melanie and I have been talking, and last year when I took over the Mothers and Children Foundation, we said we'd give it a year and then see how things went. Well, the first year is past, and the foundation is going swimmingly. Almost too good to be true. It's a fulltime job, and I could do better by the foundation if I devoted all my time to it. One Way is self-sufficient, too, or could be if I handed it over to the right people. Mom, after your super consult and reorganization, it is well put together. It never should have depended upon me for so much, and I'm certainly not indispensable. I think I'm ready to entrust One Way to other hands, and devote all my time to the foundation."

Faith and Scott joined Jon congratulating Jeremy on the decision.

As the mothers and their kids filed back in, Jeremy said, "Oh, yes, Mom, I forgot to give you back your pen. Thanks for letting me use it."

EPILOGUE: LAKE COMPANION

After driving home from Oak Park, Scott and Faith were relaxing in front of the window, sitting in their matching recliners. It had been chilly, so she made them some hot chocolate. The evening gradually descended upon Chicago, but neither of them turned on a light as they watched the curtain of night fall on the lake.

"Scott, I have a confession to make."

"You're supposed to say, 'Bless me, Father, for I have sinned.'"

"This is a different kind of confession. Not a sin, a secret."

"Fine. I can keep a secret."

"Scott, all those years when I was alone, I liked to walk along the lake, and it seemed to...well, not talk to me, but share my misery, make me feel better. I made the lake my constant companion, and after I moved here, I liked to do what we're doing now, leave the lights off, and just commune with the lake."

"Same confession for me. I've always loved the lake, too. Like you, I lived alone for quite a while. Sometimes it got depressing. Whenever my spirits ran low, a walk along the beach would cheer me up. Even in the cold of winter."

They looked out over the water. The sky was dusted with cotton ball clouds, the water flecked with whitecaps.

"You know, Scott, the furniture companies have a trade-in program for old chairs like ours."

"I thought you liked these loungers."

"I do. But they've got a new one, a 'cuddler.' Just big enough for two people to sit next to each other."

He smiled.

"Cuddle.

Count the stars.

Commune with the lake."

ACKNOWLEDGMENTS

I would like to thank the people who listened to, and read, early drafts of this novel includingPeter Berkos and the Rancho Bernardo Writers Group, Mike Sirota, and Caroline McCullagh.

I would also like to thank my publisher, Rick Lakin, at iCrew Digital Publishing, DJ Rogers of Justwritedesign.com for the cover.

PRAISE FOR THE TWIN DESTINY SERIES

"In *No Pizza in Heaven*, H. Byron Earhart uses his vast knowledge of comparative religion to craft a compelling study of how belief can both destroy and heal."

— RICHARD LEDERER, BEST-SELLING AUTHOR OF
BOOKS ABOUT LANGUAGE AND HISTORY

Faith Finds Forgiveness

In *Faith Finds Forgiveness*, H. Byron Earhart's fine follow-up to *No Pizza in Heaven*, Faith Armstrong attempts to reconcile her life by seeking out the man who fathered her twin sons during one night of passion so long ago. Readers of the Twin Destiny series will not be disappointed.

— MIKE SIROTA

This book is a page-turner. I only read when I take naps or hit the sack, and last night I finished the book by staying up late.

Love the new character, Father Whitmore. He's a good guy and represents a good Episcopal church. He neve dragged Faith this way or that, he merely listened to her when she needed an ear. I almost thought he and Faith would end up together.

I got to know Doug more in this book, and he is everything Faith thought he'd be. I didn't agree with her decision about him, but that's what builds a good story. If a writer can make you feel good and upset you, they have talent.

Glad to see that Faith finds happiness with her extended family, and that's all I'll say about that. Can't give away the whole story. It's a good read, and I'll start on the third book in a few days. Happy page-turning…

We follow successful career woman Faith through a self-examination of her life and the role of forgiveness for her. She examines many aspects of forgiveness as it pertains to herself: forgiveness of a strict, punitive father; forgiveness of a meek mother; forgiveness of herself for becoming pregnant as a teenager; forgiveness of the man who impregnated her; forgiveness of herself by her twin sons, now adult, who were adopted by different families and grew up not knowing one another or their birth mother; forgiveness in her religion. Ultimately, she is able to accept pleasure in life after forgiveness of others and of herself (redemption is intimated but not stressed).

Faith is presented as a successful but emotionally damaged women who examines and corrects her life's course and is able to find a much more rewarding path for herself and others. The reader finds Faith believable and finds her self-examination interesting.

Faith's quest for forgiveness is matched only by her professional expertise which becomes a part of her spiritual journey. This journey is especially challenging when she faces decisions about the twins' father.

The reader is drawn convincingly into her struggle and the conflicting emotions that result after she takes action. Faith's saga examines religious beliefs, soul-searching, and the power of understanding and compromise when finding common ground. This is a thought-provoking read that leaves one fully satisfied.

— LT

"Faith Finds Forgiveness" is Volume II of the Twin Destiny Series. After being reunited with her twin boys after many years of searching, finding much happiness now with her children and grandchildren, Faith still feels guilty about the way everything evolved and still emotionally unforgiving toward her father for the way he forced her into giving her babies up for adoption and separating them through different adoption agencies. Faith seeks spiritual counsel to resolve her many past issues, including getting away from her religious upbringing. She needs this guidance to rid herself of these demons and to get on with her life in a meaningful and spiritual way. The reader will be happy with Faith's life changing decisions. This volume is not as fast paced as Volume 1 but nevertheless is very credible due to the well-defined characters as being ordinary people that we can all relate to.

— SUE S.

A very satisfying follow up to *No Pizza in Heaven*. Faith connects with a charismatic church counselor who helps her face the issues that plague her, and at the same time she expands her relationships with her new family. Then there is the question of the father of her twins. This, and another new relationship, make for a compelling story. I recommend it.

— FRED

ABOUT H. BYRON EARHART

H. Byron Earhart, born in central Illinois, attended Knox College, and received a doctorate in History of Religions from the University of Chicago and was awarded a grant as a Fulbright Scholar. He began writing fiction as a teenager, but as a professor at Western Michigan University, published books on religion, especially religion in Japan. After retiring to San Diego, he returned to his early love of writing fiction. This is his first published novel and is Book One of the Twin Destiny Series.

Visit his websites at byronearhart.com and byronearhartauthor.com

h.byron.earhart@wmich.edu

www.ingramcontent.com/pod-product-compliance
Lightning Source LLC
Chambersburg PA
CBHW072217170626
46813CB00003B/977